MRS. MALORY AND A DEATH IN THE FAMILY

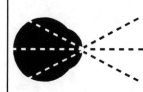

This Large Print Book carries the
Seal of Approval of N.A.V.H.

A SHEILA MALORY MYSTERY

Mrs. Malory and a Death in the Family

Hazel Holt

THORNDIKE PRESS

An imprint of Thomson Gale, a part of The Thomson Corporation

THOMSON

GALE

Detroit • New York • San Francisco • New Haven, Conn. • Waterville, Maine • London

THOMSON
GALE ™

Thorndike Press® Large Print Mystery.

The text of this Large Print edition is unabridged.

Other aspects of the book may vary from the original edition.

Set in 16 pt. Plantin.

LIBRARY OF CONGRESS CATALOGING-IN-PUBLICATION DATA

Holt, Hazel, 1928–
  Mrs. Malory and a death in the family : a Sheila Malory mystery / by Hazel Holt.
    p. cm. — (Thorndike Press large print mystery)
  ISBN-13: 978-0-7862-9456-5 (alk. paper)
  ISBN-10: 0-7862-9456-6 (alk. paper)
  1. Malory, Sheila (Fictitious character) — Fiction. 2. Women detectives — England — Fiction. 3. England — Fiction. 4. Cousins — Crimes against — Fiction. 5. Large type books. I. Title.
  PR6058.O473M745 2007
  823'.914—dc22   2006101181

Published in 2007 by arrangement with NAL Signet,
a member of Penguin Group (USA) Inc.

Printed in the United States of America on permanent paper
10 9 8 7 6 5 4 3 2 1

For Zelda
To keep it in the family

CHAPTER ONE

I am very much afraid [*my cousin Hilda wrote*] that you may have to suffer a visit from Bernard Prior. He arrived at my house uninvited, and indeed unannounced, last Wednesday and stayed for several hours. He seemed oblivious to my hints that he and that dim little wife of his had long outstayed their welcome, so that in the end I was obliged to be quite *brisk* in my effort to get rid of them.

Apparently now that he has retired he has taken up genealogy — such a tedious study, I always think — and wished to glean from me any information I might have about our common ancestors. Appalled as I was at the mere thought of having anything at all in common with Bernard Prior, I made it quite clear that I had nothing to say to him. Unfortunately this did not, as I had hoped, send him on his way. Instead he insisted on telling me at great and boring length what he had already discovered, all of which involved unfolding cumbersome family trees all over the floor, which greatly upset Tolly, who, not unnaturally, considers that to be his own particular domain. . . .

There were several more pages in this vein, a sure sign that Hilda was very put out indeed, since her letters are usually brief and to the point and go beyond one page only when her feelings (quite rarely) get the better of her. I did see what she meant, though. Bernard Prior is a first cousin on my father's side, and on the few occasions I've met him, I've resolved never willingly to repeat the experience. Not only is he a dreadful bore, but, like nearly all bores, he is convinced that people are delighted to see him, and he is very difficult indeed to shake off. Since Hilda's manner, even to her friends, verges on the acerbic, I could imagine only too well what her "briskness" had been like. The fact that he had upset her beloved Siamese, Tolly, would have made her even more formidable than usual. Not, I imagine, that even that would have penetrated Bernard's carapace of self-satisfaction.

Before he retired he was the headmaster

of a private school in Bristol, and like some — though mercifully not all — headmasters, he had acquired a tiresomely didactic tone. I always felt that he was addressing me as if I was one of his less intelligent pupils. I mentioned Hilda's letter to Michael when he rang to ask whether I'd look after Alice one evening.

"We have this tedious dinner thing we really ought to go to," he said, "and we thought you might like to spend a little time with your granddaughter."

"Of course I'd love to," I replied, "and apart from anything else, I plan to be out as much as possible in the immediate future in case Bernard suddenly turns up."

"From what I remember of Bernard," Michael said grimly, "nothing short of emigration will save you from a visit by him. My childhood was blighted by one ghastly afternoon when he went on interminably about steam railways he had visited."

"Goodness, yes, I remember that. By the time he finally went, I was quite *rigid* with boredom. It's genealogy this time and, from what Hilda said, it looks as if he wants some *input* from the rest of the family."

"Well," Michael advised, "don't get the photographs out, whatever you do; otherwise, you'll never get rid of him."

"What I particularly dislike about him," I said thoughtfully, "is the way he just turns up without any warning. One time he and Janet arrived just after midday and he simply ignored the fact that we were in the middle of lunch. I did offer them something, but he waved it away and simply carried on talking about whatever he was mad about then, while I was clearing the half-eaten food from the table. Janet looked really embarrassed, but I suppose, poor soul, she must be used to it by now. Anyway, she obviously adores him and thinks he's marvelous — well, she must have, else she couldn't have stood it all these years."

"All I can say is, the best of luck," Michael said. "So what about Tuesday? Thea said she'll give Alice her supper before we go so it'll be just bath and bedtime story. OK?"

My friend Rosemary was equally sympathetic.

"Oh, poor you; how vile! I *do* know what you mean. Every family has one. Ours is Uncle Ernest's youngest son, Tim. He could bore for England — he's sports mad and knows the date and score of every cricket match since the year dot. Poor Jack, who's keen enough on cricket, goodness knows, turns pale at the thought of him. He lives in Manchester, thank goodness, so we don't see that much of him, and fortunately Mother was really rude to him last time he was down here, so perhaps she'll have put him off."

"Hilda was very rude to Bernard," I said with a sort of melancholy pride, "but it didn't seem to have any effect on him at all."

"Oh, well," Rosemary said. "Perhaps you can palm him off onto other relations — you've got a fair number of cousins and whatnot, and some of them live quite near."

"That's a thought," I said gratefully. "There's Cousin Richard and his family, who're just the other side of Taunton, and Harry and his lot at Brendon, and poor old Fred, if he's still alive; I haven't heard from him for ages. Though, of course, since he lives in Bristol, Bernard may have got at him already. Oh, yes, and there's Cousin Sybil over at Lynton in that convent place. Only she's not Sybil anymore; I think she's Sister Veronica now."

"I didn't know you had a cousin in a convent," Rosemary said.

"Some sort of second cousin — I've never quite worked out the relationship," I said. "No doubt Bernard will be able to explain it to me!"

"What I meant to ask you," Rosemary said, "is do you feel like coming blackberry-ing one day? — they're very good this year and just getting properly ripe."

"I don't know," I said. "I love blackberries — well, I do when they've been put through a sieve; I can't manage those pips now — but I'm not mad about picking them. I always seem to tear my hands to pieces when I try."

"Oh, do come," Rosemary urged. "We can take a flask and make an afternoon of it. There are always some gorgeous ones up above Robbers Bridge, and it'll be lovely there now the tourists have gone and it's all peaceful."

"Well, I suppose I could always wear some gloves . . ."

"Bless you. I want to make some sloe and blackberry jelly, so I'll need quite a lot, and I couldn't face going off to pick them on my own. It's supposed to be a nice day tomorrow, so shall I come for you just after two?"

It was a perfect autumn afternoon, quite warm, with gleams of bright sunlight coming and going from behind the clouds. We made our way along the hedgerows bordering the track above the river, picking as we went.

"They're nice and ripe," Rosemary said, "but not too squashy."

"And," I said thankfully, "there are quite a few at eye level — I do so hate it when you have to pull down the sprays with the best ones on and they spring back and hit you in the face! They're just about perfect just now; much later and the devil would be in them — isn't that what they say?"

"Mm, yes. I must say," Rosemary went on, "there's something immensely satisfying about gathering things from the hedgerows — sort of *traditional,* what people have always been doing."

"And free," I said. "That makes it even better. When we were small we used to pick the hazelnuts too, do you remember? There never seem to be any now. I wonder why."

"I suppose the squirrels have them, and there are probably more squirrels now, like there are more rats in towns. Do you know, the last time I was in London I saw a rat in Leicester Square."

"No! Really?"

"Yes, it was sitting up on the pavement, bold as brass, absolutely unconcerned, and none of the passersby took any notice of it. I was appalled."

When our plastic boxes were full, we went back to the car.

"It's really quite warm," Rosemary said. "Shall we have our tea by the river? I've got a rug somewhere in the boot."

Sitting with our cups and slices of Rosemary's delicious chocolate cake, we watched the dragonflies swooping over the river — hardly more than a stream here — while a buzzard hovered over the bracken-covered slopes of the hills behind us.

"Yes," Rosemary said, reverting to her earlier theme, "traditional — really timeless, like this valley. It doesn't look as if it's changed for hundreds of years. People must have been coming here for centuries, hunting and gathering and whatever they did. Our remotest ancestors —" She broke off and laughed. "Perhaps you'd better send your cousin Bernard out here to get in touch with them."

"Don't remind me," I said. "I've been trying to put it out of my mind."

But it seemed that I was fated not to do so. A few days later I had a letter from another cousin (my grandfather was one of eight children, so there are a multiplicity of cousins both close and remote), Marjorie, who lives in Kirkby Lonsdale.

You will be interested to hear [*she wrote*] that I have just had a visit from our cousin Bernard and his wife. They were on a caravanning holiday in the Lakes and said they felt they must look me up as they were so near. Bernard has taken up genealogy, such a fascinating study I always think, and is most anxious to talk to as many members of the family as possible. He was most interested in all the old photographs I have and borrowed some of them to take away and have copies made. I said I was afraid some of them were sadly faded, but he said they can do wonderful things with them nowadays. He was really delighted to learn that I still had some of the letters your Great Uncle John wrote to your Grandmother in the First World War, and, of course, the letter and the citation they sent her when he was killed.

I told him that your father had inherited the big family Bible with all the dates in it and I said I was sure you would be delighted to show it to him and any other family things that you may have. He said that now he has retired he plans to spend some time in the West Country "rediscovering the family roots," as he put it. It was so nice to see him and Janet again. They stayed for several hours and Bernard came back the following morning to check on a few things he'd forgotten to ask.

"*Bother* Marjorie!" I said to Michael when I went round to babysit Alice. "She's a dear soul, but she does love company — any company — and she obviously had a lovely time listening to Bernard boring on, but I do wish she hadn't passed him on to me!"

"Well, you'll just have to be brisk with him too, like Hilda," Michael said.

"You know I can't do that. I'm hopeless at being rude to people. There are several people — people I would gladly never see again — and all it would take would be one really beastly remark and I'd be free of them forever, but somehow I just can't do it."

"Do what?" asked Thea, coming into the room with Alice.

"Be really rude to people I dislike so that I don't have to see them again."

"Oh, I *do* know what you mean," she agreed. "You want to so much, but the words simply won't come!"

Alice, who had been impatiently waiting to attract my attention, tugged at my arm and said, "The book, Gran; have you brought the book? You promised."

"I hope you have," Thea said. "She's been

16

talking about nothing else since she got back from nursery school today."

"Of course I have. Linda sent it specially for you, Alice, all the way from America."

"America!" Alice echoed, the word obviously having no meaning for her. "Read it now!"

"When you've had your bath and are in bed."

Alice rushed towards the stairs. "Come on, Gran!"

"I've left some sandwiches and things in the kitchen, and help yourself to drinks and whatever. Oh, yes, and the telephone number's on the kitchen table. We should be back about ten thirty —"

"Come along, Thea!" said Michael, as impatient as his daughter. "Ma knows where everything is — we'll be late."

Thea gave me an apologetic smile and disappeared after him.

When I had read *The Moose in the House* to Alice (three times) and she was finally settled and asleep, I looked down at my granddaughter and wished, as I so often did, that my husband, Peter, and my mother were still alive and could have seen her. I stood there for a while, thinking of parents and children, going back generation after generation. I've never really understood about genes, but I thought of how little bits of people who had gone before were present in their descendants and felt that, somehow, something of Peter and my mother were there in the sleeping form before me. It was a comforting thought, and I smiled and pulled the coverlet more tidily over Alice. Leaving the door slightly ajar, I went downstairs to my smoked salmon sandwiches and my copy of *Mapp and Lucia.*

Possibly the same mood was still with me the next day, because I was moved to open the glass-fronted bookcase in the sitting room (where the "special" books had always been kept) and take out the big family Bible. I noticed somewhat guiltily that the leather binding was beginning to crumble at the corners and made a resolution to rub in some lanolin (could one still get lanolin?) to try to restore it. The leather was embossed with a pattern, and it was still possible to read the lettering round the circle in the middle: SOCIETY FOR PROMOTING CHRISTIAN KNOWLEDGE. I laid it on the table in the dining room, because it was too heavy to hold, and opened it.

On the flyleaf in Gothic lettering were the words *Samuel Prior: His Book: November 18th 1830,* presumably the date of his confirmation. Inside the cover there was a long list, covering both sides, recording the births of generations of my father's family, beginning with *Mary Prior, born at nine o'clock on the evening of September 10th 1846.* The writing was brown and faded but still clear enough to read. The entries ended with the record of my father's birth, and I felt a faint sense of disappointment that I was not included in that list. Taking down the Bible that had belonged to my father, I saw that he had recorded the date of his marriage to my mother and the dates of birth of my brother and myself. Under the entry for my brother, the date of his death, together with the words *In action in Cyprus,* was neatly written.

I sat for quite a while, not really looking at the volumes before me, but absorbing, as it were, the information they contained. Then I shut them, put them away, and went into the kitchen to cook some of the black-berries I'd picked with Rosemary. Foss, my Siamese, attracted by the sound of someone in the kitchen, materialized suddenly and, leaping up onto the work-top, began his inevitable demands for food. Tris, who had been sleeping peacefully in his dog basket, decided he was missing something and joined in with short, excited barks. Brought back to reality and the present day, I opened tins for them both and put the radio on just in time for a talk on divorce settlements on *Woman's Hour.*

I'd just finished putting the blackberries through a sieve (extraordinary how little you're left with from a whole lot of berries) when the phone rang. It was my friend Anthea.

"It's about the talk for the over-sixties at Brunswick Lodge," she said, and my heart sank because I knew that meant she wanted me to do something about it.

"What's happened?"

"That woman who was coming to talk to them about nutrition — you know, the one from the complementary medicine place — well, she's suddenly said she can't come."

"Oh, dear, why not?"

"Some silly excuse about having to go to a conference in Amsterdam. Apparently one of her *team* — whatever that might be! — has dropped out, so she says she's got to go instead. I said surely she could tell them she had a previous engagement, but she said it was very important. So irresponsible! And what are they doing going to Amsterdam, anyway? The last place, I should think — eating nothing but cheese — all that cholesterol!"

"So are you having to cancel it?"

"Of course not — we can't let all those people down. No, I wondered if you could think of anyone who'd fill in."

"I suppose Barry could do his local history thing again."

"Certainly not. He was absolutely hopeless last time — kept losing his place in his notes and repeating himself; most embarrassing."

"What about someone from Age Concern?"

"No, I've tried them. They haven't anyone available until November."

"I'm afraid I can't think of anyone else."

"I don't suppose you —"

"No," I said firmly. "I hate speaking in public."

"But you give papers at conferences," Anthea said persuasively.

"That's quite different. Anyway, I haven't anything suitable prepared and I haven't the time to do anything new."

"It doesn't have to be *suitable*," Anthea said, but she knew she was fighting a battle she couldn't win. We've been over this ground many times, and although in general I can never stand up to her, on this subject I've managed to remain firm.

"Oh, well, it does seem a pity," Anthea said disconsolately. "Give me a ring if you think of anybody."

After this encounter I felt so exhausted that before going back to my blackberries I made myself a strong cup of tea. When I was sitting drinking it, on an impulse, I got up and took out my father's Bible again. On the flyleaf I added the dates of my parents' deaths, my marriage to Peter, the date of his death, the date of Michael's birth and marriage and, finally, that of the birth of Alice.

"There," I said to no one in particular when I'd finished, "that's better."

CHAPTER TWO

One of the jobs I really hate doing is taking all the crockery and glassware from the dresser in the kitchen, washing it, and putting it all back again. I try to do it twice a year, but this year I'd resolutely closed my eyes to it and, as a result, when a particularly strong ray of sunshine came through the window and focused on the open shelves, I was appalled to see how badly it all needed doing. With a sigh I began to take the plates and dishes off the shelves and stack them on the kitchen table. Although I hardly ever fry anything nowadays, there was an unpleasant film on everything from that mysterious, invisible grease that seems to hang in the air of even the best-regulated kitchen — and goodness knows, no one would ever describe my kitchen like that.

Because some of the china was old (some of it my mother's, some, even, my grandmother's), I had to wash it all by hand, so I filled the sink with warm, soapy water, switched the radio on, and set to work. Once I got down to it, I quite enjoyed the pleasure you can get from a mindless task. The noise of the front doorbell cut sharply through the mellifluous sound of Delius's "Walk to the Paradise Garden." I made an exclamation of annoyance and went to answer it, still wearing my apron and rubber gloves. On the doorstep were Bernard and Janet Prior.

"We were in the area," Bernard said, "and felt we must call and see you."

"You'd better come in," I said and led the way into the sitting room. "Sit down," I said grudgingly, "while I just go and turn the radio off."

I went into the kitchen and removed my rubber gloves and apron, turned off the radio, cast a glance at the table full of crockery and the sink full of soapy water, both of which now seemed infinitely attractive, and went slowly back into the sitting room.

They were sitting side by side on the sofa, and I saw, with apprehension, that Bernard had already opened the briefcase he had with him and was laying various papers out onto the small table beside him.

"How long are you down here for?"
I asked.

"I'm not sure yet," Bernard said, still sorting through the papers. "It all depends on how much material there is."

"Material?" I inquired innocently.

"Yes, didn't Marjorie write to you? She said she was going to do so; she was really enthusiastic about my project."

"I believe she did say something about you doing a sort of family tree."

"Oh, *much* more than that," Bernard said reprovingly, giving me what I always thought of as his "headmasterly stare." "What I intend to do is to make what is virtually a family history, going right back as far as records will take me."

"I wouldn't have thought," I said provocatively, "that our family was of sufficient importance to have *that* sort of treatment."

He gave me the stare again as if I was a recalcitrant pupil. "But, my dear Sheila," he said, "it is precisely our sort of family — not of the highest echelons of society, not known to the world in general, but of good, solid stock, the backbone, you might say, of England — that should be chronicled in this fashion."

I didn't say anything and he went on. "I have, of course, thoroughly investigated my

25

branch of the family down from our common grandfather, but since my father was one of seven children there is a great deal to do concerning his siblings. Then," he continued, "when I have fully established exactly what information we have about those descendants, I will go back from our grandfather to previous generations."

"It sounds like a lot of work," I said, "but I suppose you've got time on your hands now you're retired."

"One makes time for what is important," Bernard said. "As a matter of fact, I do a certain amount of charitable work as well as being a lay preacher at my local church."

"How splendid," I said, thinking with pity of the objects of his charity and the members of his congregation.

"Now, then," he said, taking out a pair of spectacles, "I believe you have the family Bible with certain entries that I may not have."

Reluctantly I got to my feet to fetch it, knowing that this would all take a very long time.

"I'll put it on the large table," I said, "since it is so heavy."

"Excellent. Janet," he went on, "will be making notes for me as we go along so that I will have an accurate record of all the information at our disposal."

Sure enough, Janet had a notebook and pen at the ready, and I moved away from the table so that she could join him there.

"Would you like a cup of tea or coffee?" I asked.

"Herbal tea if you have it," Bernard said. "No milk, no sugar."

"I think I've got some somewhere. For you too, Janet?" I asked.

She nodded but didn't vouchsafe an audible answer.

I found a box of peppermint tea bags at the back of one of the cupboards, relic of a bout of indigestion a year ago. I sniffed them and they still smelled fairly minty, so I thought they'd be all right. As a sort of gesture I made myself a cup of hot chocolate. I lingered in the kitchen as long as I could, but eventually I took the tray into the sitting room.

They had made themselves quite at home, sitting on either side of the table, Janet writing busily while he called out the names and dates of past generations of Priors.

"I hope peppermint tea is all right," I said as I put the tray down. Bernard waved me away and went on with his task. Repressing an impulse to back into the kitchen and leave them to it, I sat down and slowly drank my hot chocolate.

"There seems to be some discrepancy here," Bernard said, looking up and fixing me with a stern glance. "My records have 1867 as the date for William Prior's birth," he said. "Here it is given as 1869."

"Oh, is it?" I said. "I suppose one of them must be wrong."

"Obviously. Do you have any idea why the date here should be different?"

"I haven't the faintest idea," I said.

"Did your father say anything that might be relevant?"

"I don't think we ever talked about it, really."

Bernard made an impatient exclamation and I felt obliged to make some sort of comment.

"I suppose there could have been two Williams. I mean, children — children of large families — often died young and the parents sometimes used the same name for the next child. It happens occasionally in Victorian novels," I said helpfully.

He regarded me thoughtfully for a moment. "It is a possibility. I will bear it in mind."

"Do drink your tea, Janet," I said, "before it gets cold."

She looked at Bernard as if for approval

and then got up and fetched the cups from the tray.

"I hope it's as you like it." I said.

"It's lovely," she replied, sipping it quickly as if anxious to get back to her task.

He drank his more slowly, looking round the room. "That," he said nodding in the direction of a photograph on the bureau, "is your father, of course, and that is your mother. Now, she was a Gray, was she not? A local family, I believe."

"Exeter," I said. "Not exactly local."

"I see."

Janet made another entry in her notebook, which somehow annoyed me. "Anyhow," I said, "that's not relevant, is it?"

"All connections are relevant," Bernard said sternly. "The connections of families by marriage can be vitally important."

"Hardly in our case," I protested. "It's not like alliances in noble families!"

"I think you underestimate the scope of my work. I intend to spread my net wide."

I relapsed into what I fear was sulky silence — Bernard has that effect on me — and they worked on, slowly and meticulously. I was amazed that copying the information from two leaves of the Bible should be taking so long, but every so often Bernard would stop and compare the information there with some of his own notes. I listened, for want of something better to do, to the ticking of the clock, and when it struck half past twelve I could bear it no longer.

"I'm so sorry," I said brightly, "but I'm afraid I've got to turn you out now. I've got a lunch appointment at one o'clock and, as you see" — I gestured to my old skirt — "I've got to get changed."

Bernard looked up. "Oh, dear, then we will have to continue another day — that is a pity. I had hoped to have all this information before we go to the County Record Office in Taunton."

"Some other day," I said, carefully not specifying which one. "I'm a bit busy this week. Where are you staying? Perhaps I could let you know when I'm free."

"We usually have our caravan, but since we may be down here for some time and caravan parks are not always open at this time of the year, we are renting a cottage just outside Dunster. However, it will be easiest if I leave you my mobile number." He gestured to Janet, who scribbled a number on her notebook, tore out the page, and silently gave it to me.

I got up to take it and remained standing, hoping that it would impress upon them the need to go. Finally, when all the papers were back in the briefcase, Bernard stood up.

"Well, I will hope to hear from you soon, Sheila," he said, looking regretfully at the Bible lying on the table. "It is a great pity there was not time for me to complete that stage of my research. Perhaps when I come again you will be kind enough to look out any photographs that may be relevant."

"Yes, of course," I said ushering them out into the hall. "I'll see what I can find, though I'm not sure what I've got — I'm afraid I'm very disorganized."

Bernard made no reply, but his silence was eloquent.

I went out with them to their car, less for politeness than for a desire to make sure they were really going.

"Thank you for the tea," Janet said. And, mercifully, they were gone.

I went back slowly into the house. The animals, who, prompted by some mysterious instinct, had made themselves scarce during the visit, suddenly reappeared and demanded food and attention.

"Where were you when I needed you?" I asked them. "I'm sure they're the sort of people who are allergic to animal fur."

They followed me hopefully into the kitchen, where the piles of crockery and the sink full of cold water were a dismal sight. I fed the animals and poured myself a large glass of sherry before addressing the task ahead of me.

"I really did behave rather badly," I said to Michael and Thea when I was telling them about it. "Not rude, exactly, but as unhelpful as I could be."

"I don't suppose he noticed," Michael said. "He's got a hide like a rhinoceros."

"No, I don't suppose he did," I agreed, "but it was still bad manners. And not really fair to poor Janet. It's not her fault her husband's a tiresome bore."

"I expect she's used to it. Anyway, Ma, for goodness' sake, don't let him anywhere near us."

"He's determined to talk to *all* members of the family," I said.

"Don't you dare!"

"Does he have any family?" Thea asked.

"I believe there's a son and a daughter. I seem to remember that he doesn't get on well with one of them, but I can't remember which. Mind you, I don't imagine he was particularly easy to get on with — it could be difficult to be the child of a headmaster at the best of times, and I imagine he'd have been pretty dire."

"Poor little beasts," Michael said. "Still, I suppose they're both grown-up now. Perhaps they've escaped."

"Actually," Thea said, "a basic family tree would be quite interesting."

"Oh, yes, I'm all for that, but not done by someone like Bernard and not in the sort of detail he seems to be going in for. No, a straightforward family tree would be nice. Useful too for Alice, for the years ahead when she has to do a project on it at school — I gather it's a very popular thing with them nowadays."

"Both my grandparents died when I was quite little," Thea said, "and Daddy never talked about the family, especially after Mummy died, and now — well, I see him so rarely and it's never a suitable time to bring the subject up."

"I know," I said. "I often wish I'd asked my parents more, but you always think there's plenty of time for things like that, and then, quite suddenly, there isn't."

"Oh, well," Thea said. "I'll put the kettle on, shall I? There's just time for a quick cup of tea before I have to go and collect Alice."

The phone was ringing as I opened the door, and I made a dash for it, nearly falling over Tris, who'd come to welcome me.

After all that effort, it was only Anthea.

"Have you had any more thoughts?" she asked.

"Thoughts about what?" I asked when I'd got my breath back.

"The over-sixties talk," Anthea said impatiently. "Have you thought of anyone? The time's going on and we have to make a decision soon. Now," she went on coaxingly, "are you really sure you won't —"

"Absolutely sure," I said firmly. "No, hang on a minute, I've had an idea. I might just be able to persuade someone I know to give a talk on genealogy. It's very popular now, especially with people who've just retired; they're all mad to trace their ancestors."

"Who is this person?"

"A sort of cousin of mine," I said. "He lives in Bristol, actually, but he's down here for a bit doing some research, and I might be able to persuade him to stay on and help us out."

"It might do, I suppose." Anthea was never one to be enthusiastic about other people's ideas.

"He's an ex-headmaster," I said temptingly, "so he's very used to addressing large gatherings."

"Well, all right, then," Anthea said grudgingly. "See what you can do about it and get back to me."

I smiled as I put down the phone. If I managed to arrange things and the talk was a success, I knew very well that Anthea would claim the credit for it all. Still, if Bernard gave the talk, that would get Anthea off my back. I knew from bitter experience that she could, over a period of time, wear me down, and I really didn't want the time-consuming bother of preparing something suitable for the over-sixties. Of course, I knew that ringing Bernard about the talk meant that I'd have to arrange a date for him to visit me again, but I felt that it was a reasonable price to pay. And, in a way, I felt a bit guilty about the offhand way I'd behaved when he came before. I could hear my mother's voice reminding me that politeness costs nothing.

Needless to say, when I went to look for it I couldn't find the piece of paper with Bernard's mobile number on it, but I finally ran it to earth shut up in the family Bible — the obvious place to have looked, I suppose. When I dialed the number, Bernard answered right away — obviously one of those people who *expect* to be rung and are poised to respond immediately.

"Bernard, it's Sheila. I just wondered, will

you be here on the nineteenth?"

"Quite probably. Why do you ask?"

I explained about the over-sixties and how interested they all were in genealogy and said how they'd be thrilled to have the benefit of his advice on the technique of tracing their ancestors, and how he would be the perfect person to talk to them, and so on, and so forth. To my delight, he took the bait straightaway.

"Yes, I think I could manage that date," he said. "I very much doubt if I will have finished my research down here before then, and I do feel it is very important, as I think I said to you, that we should all be aware of our family histories. Perhaps you would be good enough to fill me in on the details — time and place, of course, and the length and scope of the talk. We can discuss it at more length when I visit you."

"Yes, of course," I said, "and it's so good of you to agree. I know everyone will be most excited." I paused for a moment, but knew I had to go on. "It would be lovely to see you and Janet next Monday — about two thirty, if that suits you? I'll see what photos I can dig out."

"That will be excellent. I am aiming to make it a pictorial record as far as possible."

"That's fine, then," I said. "I'll look

forward to seeing you both." I put the phone down.

"And don't look at me like that," I said to Tris, who was regarding me quizzically with his head on one side. "If it weren't for white lies, the world would almost certainly grind to a halt."

CHAPTER THREE

I do wish I was the sort of person who puts photographs into albums. Mine — the more recent ones, anyway — are stuffed into shoe boxes or even lie, curled up at the edges, loose in drawers. My father used to be very conscientious about his photographs. I can see him now, sitting at the table with a box of "photograph corners," as they were called, sticking them onto the pages of the album and then painstakingly sliding each photograph neatly into them. Of course, in those days, people took fewer pictures. Each exposure was carefully considered; there was no quick *click, click, click* that people go in for now, taking a whole series of pictures to get one particular shot. My father would have considered that dreadfully wasteful.

Our old family photos — the formal, framed ones — hang in the spare room and what I still thought of as Michael's room. I unhooked them from the walls and laid them on the bed — sepia representations not just of people but of a vanished way of life. I took up the group photograph of my grandparents and their children. It was probably taken a few years before the Great War, possibly the last time the whole family was together: my grandfather, bearded and stern looking, my grandmother in her best silk dress with elegant pintucking down the front and her pince-nez on a gold chain pinned to her bosom, the younger boys in sailor suits, the girls with their hair freshly brushed into ringlets and, standing at the back, John, nearly a man, so soon to be off to war, and killed so young on the western front.

They all looked so solemn, aware of the novelty of being photographed. I smiled as I remembered what my father, the youngest of the boys, had told me once, looking at the picture: how difficult it had been to keep the boys sitting still for the length of time they had to wait while the picture was being taken, and how he'd nearly spoiled it by shouting out when his brother Arthur had pinched him at a critical moment. My father was dead now and so was Arthur, far away in Australia.

There was another photograph of John, in uniform just before he left for France. He was standing beside Sarah, the pretty girl he had married just six months before. He never lived to see his son. All the pictures of this period, formally posed, made their subjects somehow unreal, misleadingly so, since I could just remember the stern paterfamilias of the group photograph as a jolly, laughing grandfather, cheerfully indulgent and willing to play childish games with me and my brother. The pictures of my parents were more casual and so more human. I looked with affection at one of them in the early days of their marriage, leaning one on each side of the old Lagonda that was my father's pride and joy.

I gathered them all up and took them downstairs for Bernard to look at. I felt a little reluctant, somehow, to expose them to what I thought of as Bernard's critical gaze. Of course, most of them were his relations too, but because I didn't like him I suppose I felt they would dislike him too.

Monday came all too soon. I had an early lunch so that I'd have everything cleared away before they arrived, but even so they arrived a good quarter of an hour early, when I was just about to treat Foss for a tick that he'd picked up in his perambulations through the long grass of the surrounding fields. I shut Foss into the kitchen while I went to let them in.

"Oh, good," I said as I led them into the sitting room. "You're just in time to give me a hand. Can one of you hold my cat while I deal with a tick on his neck? It's so much easier with two."

Janet looked apprehensively at Bernard, who was spreading out the papers from his briefcase on the table. I got the impression that she was appalled that anyone had had the temerity to expect him to do such a thing.

"I'm sure Janet will be pleased to help you," he said, not looking up from his task.

"Yes, yes, of course, I'll be delighted . . ." Her voice trailed off.

"It's all right," I said reassuringly. "He's quite good — usually. I'll just go and fetch him."

I went out and gathered up an irritable Foss, brought him in, and gave him to Janet to hold. She held him confidently, lovingly, even, and I was surprised because I imagined she'd be unused to animals.

"Oh, he's a Siamese," she said. "Isn't he beautiful! My mother had a Siamese, a seal point, named Ming. He used to be able to open doors with his paw."

Since this was practically the only time I'd ever heard Janet make a remark on her own behalf, I regarded her with interest and even Foss turned his head to look at her.

"I think I've killed the tick," I said. "I put some stuff on it last night, so it should be dead by now. There it is, on his neck, just by his collar. I think I can just pull it off now." I gave it a tug with the tweezers. "Yes, it's come right away. If you're not careful, you can leave the head in and then it can be nasty."

I took Foss from her and I fancied she gave him up reluctantly.

"I'll just go and give him a treat for being good," I said, "then I'll be right back."

When I got back into the room, Bernard said, "Well, if you're *quite* ready, perhaps we might get on."

I looked at Janet sitting at the table opposite him, her notebook open and ready, once again the perfect amanuensis, and wondered whether I'd imagined the brief moment of rapport between us.

"Yes, of course," I said. "I've got the photos for you — the formal ones, anyway. I believe there's an old album somewhere, with snapshots in it. I haven't had a chance to look it out for you yet. I've got a nasty feeling it's up in the attic in one of the old suitcases there. But I will have a look. Anyway, here are the ones I expect you'd like to see." I laid them out on the sofa and he came over to look at them.

"Yes, these are certainly useful. What I would like to do is take copies of them." He reached over to the table. "Now, I do have a digital camera here," he said, producing it, "so I propose making copies with that. If, however, I cannot get the quality of reproduction I would like, I will ask you if I may borrow them so that they can be taken out of their frames and reproduced professionally. I imagine there is a competent photographic shop in Taviscombe that could do such a thing."

"Yes," I said, "there's a very good one in the Avenue."

"Good." He picked up the group photograph. "I myself have a copy of this. I believe each member of the family was given one, and mine, of course, belonged to my father." He indicated a boy of about ten dressed in a sailor suit, the collar slightly awry. He looked a pleasant child, not staring straight at the camera, as the others were, but casting a sidelong glance at what was going on somewhere out of the picture. I wondered if he had ever, in later life, cast that clear gaze upon his son, and if so, what conclusion he had drawn.

"Now," Bernard was saying, "if you could

kindly draw back the curtains so that I have the optimum light, I will see what I can do myself."

Taking the photos took a very long time. They had to be arranged, rearranged, and arranged again in different lights. The curtains had to be drawn, put back, and drawn again. Fortunately Janet did most of the arranging, but it made me feel tired just to watch her. Finally, when he had exhausted every possible combination and actually taken the photos, he called me over to look at some of them through the little sort of viewfinder at the side.

"They're very good," I said, "absolutely marvelous. It must be an exceptional camera to get that sort of result."

"It was given to me by the staff as a retirement present," he said.

"How lovely," I said, though inwardly I wondered whether the large sum of money necessary to buy such a splendid camera was an index of how delighted they all were to be rid of him!

He fiddled about with the camera for a little longer and then pronounced that some of the pictures weren't as clear as they might be so he proposed taking the originals away. I agreed readily, hoping that this might be the end of the exercise, but alas, he then produced one of his charts with names and dates and began to cross-question me about them. What little family history I did know was completely obliterated as he droned on about all the Samuels, Johns, Williams, Marys, Marthas, Janes and Louisas. It was not helped by the fact that the same names occurred in successive generations, so that after a while I was utterly confused and gave up trying to make sense of any of it.

"According to my sources it would seem that John Prior married twice," Bernard was saying, "firstly in 1865 to Charlotte Mavor, born 1847. They had issue: John, born 1866, and Edward, in" — he consulted his papers — "1868, which is the same date that Charlotte died, presumably in child-birth. He then married, in March 1872, Elizabeth Lindsey, born 1849 . . ."

But I wasn't attending. I was thinking of poor Charlotte, dying at twenty-one, leaving her little boys to be brought up by a step-mother, almost as young. I hoped Elizabeth had been as kind as the young stepmother in Charlotte M. Yonge's book.

"The entry in your Bible, however," Bernard was saying, "has the marriage taking place in *July* 1872. Can you account for this discrepancy?"

"Perhaps one of the people got it wrong,"

I suggested.

Bernard gave me a cold stare. "I will, of course, check what I can at the County Records Office. I have made an appointment to see some of the relevant material on Wednesday, but it would have been helpful if we could have settled such matters first."

"I'm very sorry," I said defensively, "but I'm afraid I've never really given much thought to any of this."

"That, so often, is the problem," Bernard said, "and that is how valuable information is lost, simply by default."

I didn't feel able to comment on this, so I said, "Oh, before I forget, I must give you the details of the talk at Brunswick Lodge. It was so good of you to help us out at such short notice. I think the best thing will be for you to have a word with Anthea Russell, who's in charge of the whole thing. I've written her address and telephone number down for you." I handed him the piece of paper and thought with some satisfaction of the conversation that would ensue: Anthea's acerbic manner versus Bernard's impervious self-satisfaction.

Fortunately, after that they did actually go, not, however, without Bernard's promising to give me the full details of his research at the County Records Office.

"How lovely," I said faintly, waving them off with false bonhomie at the front door.

I closed the door behind them, resisting a temptation to lock and bolt it in case they came back, and went and made myself the cup of tea I should have offered them but hadn't.

I spent the next few days answering the telephone cautiously in case it was Bernard. I did hear from Anthea.

"That cousin of yours doesn't half go on," she said. "I told him the talk can't be more than half an hour and then half an hour for questions. You know what the over-sixties are like. An hour is about as much as they can manage. After that they get restive and want their tea and biscuits."

"Well," I said, "you'll be in the chair, won't you, and I'm sure you'll be able to control the timing. You're always so good at that sort of thing."

Which is perfectly true. I've known Anthea to ruthlessly cut short a very eminent musicologist in full flow when she thought he'd overrun his time.

"Oh, by the way, Sheila," Anthea went on, "I don't suppose you could make a couple of your sponges. Biscuits are all right for coffee mornings, but I always feel *cake* is more suitable in the afternoon."

Feeling that I'd got off lightly from the whole affair, I agreed to make the cakes, as Anthea knew very well that I would.

When I took the sponges along to Brunswick Lodge on the afternoon of Bernard's talk, I saw that Anthea had also "persuaded" other people to provide a chocolate cake, a large ginger cake and a dozen iced fairy cakes.

"Oh, there you are, Sheila." Anthea appeared suddenly in the kitchen. "I'd like you to make the tea — if you sit at the back you can just slip out five minutes before the end and get things going."

"Yes, of course." I'd planned to sit at the back anyway and I was delighted to have valid excuse for "slipping out."

"Most of the cups are set out already," Anthea said, "but you'll need to fill the sugar bowls and get the milk out of the fridge in good time. It's such a pity," she went on, "that we haven't been able to raise funds for a new tea urn."

I made a noncommittal noise in reply, thanking heaven that I wouldn't be required to wrestle with one of those temperamental monsters. "Oh, those large teapots are fine," I said. "It's just a bit slower, that's all."

"Perhaps I'd better get Peggy Broom to help you," Anthea said, "or there'll be an immense queue and people will get restless."

"Oh, I expect I can manage."

"Well, if you're sure. I'd better go and see if Denis has put the chairs out properly."

There was a good audience for Bernard's talk; the main room was pretty well full, so I was able to be quite unobtrusive at the back. I felt that perhaps I ought to be sitting with Janet who was ensconced in the front row, but then I saw that she'd been taken over by Angela Watson, who has this thing about "making newcomers feel welcome" so I didn't need to feel guilty.

Bernard's talk was well received. I must admit that, after the first five minutes, my attention wandered and I began to think about the changes I was planning to make to my garden and the new shrubs I wanted to buy. I came to halfway through the question period to hear Bernard telling Jennifer Morris more than I'm sure she wanted to know about parish records. I made my escape into the kitchen and put the kettles on.

There was the usual scrimmage for refreshments after the talk and the usual group who always buttonhole the speaker to go on asking questions. I saw Anthea approach Bernard with a cup of tea, but, absorbed as he was with an audience, he waved her away. This didn't go down at all well, and Anthea came over to me bearing the rejected cup.

"Your cousin," she said crossly, "doesn't seem to want this tea. Perhaps you would like it." She put the cup down on the table and went away, her back registering extreme umbrage.

Raymond Poyser, who was standing nearby, moved towards me and said, "Is he your cousin, then, this Bernard Prior?"

I nodded.

"And is he the Bernard Prior who was headmaster of a school near Bristol?"

I looked at him in some surprise. "Yes, as a matter of fact, he was."

"The school," Raymond persisted, "where there was that scandal?"

"What? What scandal? I haven't heard anything about that."

"Oh, I'm sorry — perhaps I shouldn't have said anything, since he's a relation . . ."

"No, really, it's quite all right. What scandal?"

"He was cleared of all blame," Raymond said. "The parents were unhappy about the result of the inquiry, but I suppose that was only natural."

"What inquiry?" I asked. "What happened?"

"One of the boys tried to kill himself — it was all right; they found him in time, but, of course, it was all very upsetting."

"How dreadful!"

"They said he'd been bullied — well, you hear a lot about bullying now, don't you, and he was a sensitive boy, an only child and all that."

"And the staff didn't realize what was going on?"

"Partly that." Raymond paused for a moment as if considering the matter. "I think what people thought was that the headmaster didn't take that sort of thing very seriously. From what I heard, he was the sort of person who doesn't have much sympathy for people, and boys, who don't stand up for themselves."

"Yes, I can see that," I said.

"Not," Raymond said hastily, "that he was actually held responsible for what happened, but, you know how it is, people have to blame someone, and there was quite a bit about it in the local paper — I don't think it got into the nationals. I expect that's why you didn't hear about it."

"Yes, I expect so. I don't see Bernard very

often; in fact, this visit is the first time I've seen him for, goodness, it must be over fifteen years."

"He doesn't live down here, then?"

"No, he's just down here to do some research. He's renting a holiday cottage at Avill, just outside Dunster."

"I hope you didn't mind my mentioning it," Raymond said, "but I was struck by the coincidence. The boy concerned is the nephew of my neighbor, Tony Pritchard, so naturally I was interested."

"No, I'm glad you told me . . ."

Anthea reappeared at my shoulder. "Sheila, would you mind helping Peggy with the washing up? She's all alone out there." She turned to Raymond. "Just the person I wanted to see. When will you be able to move those trestles for the Bring and Buy sale?"

As I stood at the sink, automatically drying the cups and saucers that Peggy Broom was washing, I thought about what Raymond had been telling me. As a bully himself (and it was perfectly obvious to me that he *was* a bully; one glance at poor little Janet made that clear), it was no wonder that Bernard had no sympathy for the victim. He'd been extremely fortunate that there hadn't been a fatality, and I hoped he'd learned his lesson. But somehow I doubted it.

CHAPTER FOUR

Since the autumn winds had died down for the moment, I thought I really ought to get out into the garden and sweep up the leaves. It's hard work and I can only do it in short bursts, but I do quite enjoy it. I have a fair number of trees and the recent rain had brought down a lot of leaves, and as I swept I enjoyed their various shapes and colors: small yellow leaves of the silver birch that fall in showers like handfuls of golden coins, pale lemon heart-shaped leaves of the balsam, red ones from the spindle, whose cyclamen berries the birds always take before I can enjoy them; so many leaves, and all so different. It was a chilly day, but the exercise kept me warm, as, indeed, did the glow of virtue at the performance of a necessary task, and soon I had a satisfactorily big pile of leaves waiting to go onto the compost heap.

My sylvan mood was broken by sharp

barking from Tris, and I turned to find Bernard and Janet approaching me from the side gate.

"Ah, there you are," Bernard said. "There was no reply, but we assumed you were in since your car was there."

"The side gate was open," Janet said apologetically. "Oh, you have a little dog as well as your Siamese!" She stooped to stroke Tris but straightened up at a severe glance from Bernard.

"Oh, right," I said, laying aside my rake and broom, "you'd better come in."

They followed me into the house and I sent them into the sitting room while I took off my coat and boots and washed the dirt from my hands.

Bernard was back in his usual place at the table sorting out his papers, some of which he was handing to Janet, who arranged them in order.

"Now, then," he said. "I expect you would like to hear what I have been able to find out at the County Records Office. I was able to view the relevant sources and, although there were certain lacunae, I managed to piece together a fairly accurate overall picture."

"Oh, good," I said, feeling that some response was called for. Evidently it wasn't sufficient, since Bernard looked at me sternly and continued.

"They have a great deal of useful information on microfiche as well as original sources, which, having, as I think I explained to you before, made a specific appointment to do so, I was able to examine."

"Excellent," I said. This interjection was acknowledged by a slight nod.

"Now, I have drawn up a new chart, which you will like to see." He unrolled a vast sheet of paper. I got up reluctantly and went over to look at it. It certainly looked very impressive, and, given time and left to myself, I might have been able to make some sort of sense of it and even gain pleasure and information from it. Unfortunately, with Bernard instructing me in its intricacies in his most schoolmasterly manner, I soon became hopelessly lost. I was suddenly reminded of various occasions at school when a patient schoolmistress tried to explain to me the theory and practice of algebra. At such moments a kind of shutter descends in my brain, and although I may give the impression of taking in what is being said to me and even make what may sound like appropriate answers, they might just as well be addressing me in Swahili.

"So you see," Bernard was saying, "I have

been able to fill in a number of gaps — dates and even names — which were lacking before."

"That's absolutely brilliant," I said enthusiastically. "What a terrific achievement."

Bernard looked gratified at my praise, though I sensed he may have felt my language wasn't sedate enough for such a scholarly undertaking.

"Really *splendid,*" I added, that being a word that always went down well with academic colleagues.

"I have had photocopies made of the family tree and all the relevant background information I have been able to obtain," Bernard said, handing me a rolled-up document and a sheaf of papers. "One set for you and one each for Richard, Harry and Sybil. I intend visiting them within the next few days so that I can inform them about my findings. I have already seen Richard and Harry; I haven't yet completed my research on Sybil's branch of the family."

"I believe she's Sister Veronica now," I said.

"So I gather." There was an element of scorn in his voice.

"Have you been to St. Winifred's? It's a sort of nursing home in the convent. The nuns look after elderly people there. I've never actually seen it — it's tucked away in a valley the other side of Lynton."

Bernard made no comment, so I assumed he found the whole subject of Sybil's way of life distasteful. He continued, "I will send copies of my findings to Hilda and Marjorie, and Cousin Frederick I will see when I return to Bristol."

"How is he?" I asked. "It's ages since I heard from him. I had a Christmas card from him last year, but no sort of news."

"He is quite well in himself," Bernard said, "but I fear he has had a great deal of trouble with that son of his. Of course, Charles was spoiled by both of them when he was young and, after the divorce, when he went to live with Jessica, he led a very rackety sort of life — I cannot understand why she was given custody. Not that Frederick was much better, marrying again someone so much younger than himself. No," he said shaking his head, "I am afraid that is *not* a branch of our family that we can be proud of."

I wondered momentarily whether he felt proud of Michael and me.

"Oh, well," I said vaguely, "as long as he's still in the land of the living."

Bernard looked as if he was going to say something but then decided my comment wasn't worth a reply.

"Well, thank you very much for the family tree and all the other stuff," I said. "I'll look forward to studying it when I have time to look at it properly."

Prompted by the thought that this might be the last time that I saw them, I said, "Would you like a cup of tea or anything?"

"No, thank you, Sheila, we must be on our way. I have to make a visit to the church at Combe Florey, where I think there may be a gravestone that might have some relevance."

"Combe Florey," I exclaimed. "That's where the Reverend Sidney Smith was! Have you ever read his letters? The very best of nineteenth-century wit and wisdom, don't you think? I adore him — how lovely to think that our family might have had some connection with his church."

Bernard seemed unimpressed with this literary reference, merely saying that the connection, if any, would be very slight.

"When do you go back to Bristol?" I asked.

"In about ten days' time. I have a flexible arrangement with the owner of the cottage we are renting since I wasn't sure how long my research would take, and there are several things of some interest that I need to investigate further. That reminds me. I would like to keep the photographs you kindly lent me for a little longer, if that is convenient. I will, of course, return them as soon as I have finished with them."

"No, that's fine. Keep them as long as you like; they only sit there in the spare room doing nothing."

Bernard gathered up his papers and Janet shut her notebook, preparing to go.

"Oh, by the way," I said, "thank you so much for giving that talk at Brunswick Lodge. It was very much appreciated."

Bernard gave a slight smile. "I think they found something of interest in what I was saying. The study of genealogy is growing and people are increasingly aware of its importance in their lives. It is, as I am sure you would agree, fundamental to our knowledge of ourselves to be aware of the roots from which we have sprung, and it can add to our understanding not only of ourselves, but of those around us."

"Oh, absolutely," I said, knowing just how Queen Victoria felt when she said that Gladstone addressed her as if she was a public meeting. "And I'm sure Anthea was very grateful to you for stepping into the breach."

"Your friend Mrs. Russell," Bernard said repressively, "does seem to possess a very *forceful* personality. I suppose that it is necessary to adopt that somewhat abrasive manner to get things done in certain circumstances."

I smiled weakly. "She's very efficient — I don't know what Brunswick Lodge would do without her."

"Well, good-bye, Sheila. I will be in touch should I manage to glean any more information."

With this ominous promise they departed. I put the family tree and the other papers away in my desk and went outside again to finish my task, feeling that a little fresh air would help to blow away the irritated mood Bernard always left me in. Alas, while I'd been indoors the wind had got up again and my carefully garnered leaves had been blown all over the garden.

"Actually," I said to Michael and Thea the next day, "I'm sure it's all very interesting, and one day, when I have the time, I'm going to sit down and have a good look at all the stuff he left. It's just the way he goes on!"

"I hope," Michael said anxiously, "you managed to head him off from me."

"Don't worry," I said. "I know my maternal duty. He did ask about you, but I made

61

it quite clear that you had no information about the family, didn't want to know anything, and were probably about to leave the country at any minute. No, actually, it's my generation he wants to cross-question. We still have the old photos, letters and other stuff. He's right, I suppose — your generation will probably throw the whole lot out."

"Oh, come on, Ma, that's not fair. I'm really quite interested; I used to love listening to Gran's stories about when she was young, and I'd hate Alice to grow up not knowing anything about her family."

"You're lucky, really," Thea said. "I often wish I knew more about my family. One day, perhaps, when I have the time, I'll try to go into it. I believe it's much easier now that things are online."

"That's it," I said. "Time. Where does it go? I always thought that when I was older, when I was retired, I'd do all sorts of things. Read all the novels of Disraeli, things like that."

"That's the problem, though," Thea said with a smile. "Women never do retire, do they? A woman's work is never done and all that."

"Oh, come on," Michael said. "I do my bit around the house!"

"I know you do; you're very good," Thea said, "and I'm so lucky to be able to be at home all day, but still there always seems to be *something* I never get round to."

" 'All work expands to fill the time available,' " I quoted. "Which reminds me that I'd better get going if I'm going to get my shopping done before lunch." I picked up my bag and prepared to go. "It's stupid to go shopping on a Saturday — it's always so crowded — but somehow I never got around to it in the week. Time again!"

I was just considering the ripeness or otherwise of a couple of avocados (so difficult to light on the exact day when they are ripe but not going over), when someone behind me said, "Sheila! Long time no see!" I turned round to see Pam, Harry Prior's wife. "So glad I bumped into you," she continued. "We were just talking about you last night."

"Really?"

"We wondered whether this chap Bernard — some sort of cousin, isn't he? — had been in touch with you."

"Indeed he has," I said. "You too?"

Pam nodded. "You said that with feeling. Do I gather you're as fed up with him as we were?"

"Fed up is putting it mildly. The man's an

incubus!"

Pam laughed. "I'm not quite sure what an incubus is, but I'm sure he's that all right. No, honestly, he turned up at the most inconvenient time and stayed for ages. And then, just when we thought we'd got rid of him, he came *back* a couple of days later."

"He does that," I agreed, "several times. Was his wife, Janet, with him?"

"No, just him, and that was quite enough. I mean, as if we're *interested.* Poor Harry is working from morning till night — out in the fields and with the animals. Josh is at home now. He's left agricultural college and is working on the farm, but still there's always masses to do with just the two of them — we can't possible afford any full-time help; well, you know what it's like. So the last thing Harry needed was this Bernard person wittering away about family trees and census reports and stuff like that!"

"And," I said, "he's completely impervious to any sort of hint — getting rid of him is pretty well impossible."

"Exactly," Pam said. "I had to come right out and more or less ask him to go. I do bed-and-breakfast now — it's something I can do to help out the old finances — and the lot I had in wanted an evening meal, so I simply *had* to get on."

"You do have to be really rude," I said. "I couldn't *quite* manage that, but Cousin Hilda — you remember her, up in London — was. Practically told him never to darken her doors again! That saw him off."

Pam laughed. "I should jolly well think it would. I only ever met her once and I was absolutely terrified. But good for her!"

"I'm sure," I said, "that there's some quite interesting stuff in all his research, but it's something I'd like to look at, at leisure, in my own time, not with Bernard hovering over me."

"That's more or less what Harry said. This Bernard brought a lot of papers for us to see the second time he came, but Harry just shoved them in a drawer in the sideboard."

"He's still around," I said. "I'm afraid I'll have another visit from him because he's got some old photos of mine that he's got to return."

"If he comes back to us," Pam said, "Harry will go and hide with the cows and I'll pretend to be out."

I laughed. "He'll just come back again, but it's worth a try." I looked at her loaded trolley. "You've been doing a big shop. Have you still got some B and B visitors? It must be practically the end of the season for you."

She nodded. "Yes, it's almost finished now

— just one lot at the moment; then we get a bit of a surge at half term, then close down till spring, thank goodness."

"It must be really hard work," I said. "I don't know how you do it."

"Oh, well, we soldier on. It *is* pretty tiring, for all of us, really, but Harry couldn't bear to be anywhere else or do anything else. He took over from his father and he hopes Josh will take over from him."

"And do you think he will?"

"Well, Josh has always loved helping around the farm, ever since he was tiny. I don't think it's ever occurred to him to do anything else, though goodness knows how we can keep going the way things are nowadays."

"It's not a good time to be in farming," I said sympathetically. "How about Matt?" I asked. "Does he want to be a farmer too?"

"Matt? Good heavens no. He's reading law at Bristol. We hope he's going to be a highflier and restore the family fortunes. Your Michael's a solicitor, isn't he? Does he enjoy it?"

"On the whole, yes — he's working for Peter's old firm, so I suppose you could say that *he's* following in his father's footsteps too. Mind you, Thea, that's his wife, who was a solicitor too, gave up when Alice was born."

"Oh, have you got a grandchild? How marvelous. I can't wait for my two to produce offspring. How old is she?"

"She's four and a half," I said, "but very grown-up for her age." I laughed. "Oh, dear, I sound like a typical doting grandmother, don't I? But she is a great joy — I'm very lucky they live so near so that I can watch Alice grow up."

Pam looked at her watch. "Goodness, is that the time? I must get a move on. It's been great seeing you, Sheila. Do come and see us soon — it'd be good to have a proper chat. Bring Alice to see the cows."

"She'd like that, and so would I. I'll give you a ring."

As I watched Pam's tall, sturdy figure moving towards the checkout, I thought about how hard her life must be and about the effort she and Harry were making, against all the odds, to keep the farm going. Keeping it in the family. And I thought how Bernard's appearance in Taviscombe, irritating though it was, had made me think much more about families in general and my family, in all its ramifications, in particular.

CHAPTER FIVE

Every year I intend to put my bulbs in nice and early so that I'll have something flowering for Christmas, but every year, although, in a fit of enthusiasm, I buy them right at the beginning of September, they hang about in brown paper bags until I can find a moment to do something about them. To be fair, it is quite a business: getting the bulb fiber out, trying to remember where I stored the containers, and eventually covering the kitchen table with sheets of newspaper and finally getting down to it. Not helped, of course, by Foss, always passionately interested in anything unusual taking place in the kitchen. When he discovered that a hyacinth bulb was notionally round and would, propelled by an inquisitive paw, roll right off the table, and that by swishing his tail he could sweep quite large amounts of bulb fiber onto the floor, I decided that enough was enough and put him out. Turning my back on the window where his indignant face was reproaching me, I got to work.

I was just firming the earth on a bowl of jonquils when, to my annoyance, the phone rang.

Somehow I was not surprised to find that it was Bernard.

"Ah, Sheila. I am proposing to return the photographs to you this evening, together with most of the additional material I have been able to find. I say *most* because I have not yet been able to make full copies of my notes. Janet, I regret to say, has not been well these last few days and has had to stay indoors."

"I'm so sorry," I said. "I hope it was nothing serious."

"Some sort of virus, I believe," he said dismissively. "Most annoying — I have had to make all the preliminary notes from source myself, and now I am having to spend time writing them up. So I will not be able to return the photographs and the other material to you myself. Janet will bring them round to you this evening."

"This evening?"

"About eight o'clock. If," he added perfunctorily, "that is convenient for you."

"Yes," I said resignedly, "that'll be all

right. If you're sure she's quite recovered — I mean, I could collect them from you if she's still under the weather."

"No, Janet is perfectly recovered."

But when Janet arrived, right on the dot of eight, I thought she looked far from well. Normally pale and washed-out looking, she looked positively ghostlike.

"Do come in," I said. "I've got the fire on — you look frozen."

"It is quite autumnal," she said. "This heavy rain and a cold wind."

I took her coat and sat her down in a chair near the fire.

"What can I get you, to warm you up?" I asked. "Some herbal tea, or something stronger — a glass of sherry or a gin and tonic?"

"A cup of tea would be lovely, thank you so much." She held out a package. "Bernard was very anxious to get the photographs back to you safely. He was most grateful to you for letting him borrow them."

"Glad to help," I said and put the package down on the table by the window.

Just then Foss, attracted by the sound of voices, came in and made straight for Janet, leaping up onto her lap and settling down, apparently for the evening.

"Goodness," I said, "you are honored. He doesn't usually take to people he doesn't know. Do put him down if he's too much for you."

"No, no, really," she said smiling, "I'm delighted. I love cats. I often wish — but it isn't really possible . . ." She bent over and began to stroke Foss, firmly along his backbone, in just the way he likes.

As I made the tea (herbal for Janet and Indian for me), I thought how she was transformed when she smiled, and I thought with pity that she probably didn't have all that much in her life to smile about. She accepted the tea gratefully and drank it sitting awkwardly so as not to disturb Foss.

"Bernard said you haven't been well," I said. "Are you sure you're properly recovered?"

"Oh, yes, I'm fine, really — a bit weak, but nothing to speak of. Bernard" — she gave a little nervous laugh, quite different from her smile — "Bernard doesn't like me to be ill."

I bit back a retort and said, "If you're sure. You really shouldn't have come out in this weather."

"No, really, I'm perfectly well."

There was a brief silence, neither of us quite knowing what to say.

71

"When do you go back to Bristol?" I asked.

"Next week, I think, if Bernard has finished his research."

"I expect you'll be glad to be home," I said.

"Oh, yes." She seemed about to add something to this brief reply, but apparently thought better of it and sat there, quietly stroking Foss.

"I can't remember — my memory is getting really dreadful — you have two children, don't you?"

"That's right. My daughter, Christine, and my son, Luke."

"That's nice. What do they do?"

"Christine is married — Jonathan, her husband, is a financial adviser — but she teaches, like Bernard."

"Have they any children?"

"Oh, no. Christine has a very absorbing job. She's head of department at a sixth-form college, and you know what young people are like these days, putting off having a family till they're in their late thirties. So I suppose" — she gave the nervous little laugh again — "I'll have to wait for my grandchildren."

"That's a shame. Fortunately Thea — that's Michael's wife — has always longed for a family. She was a solicitor, and a very good one, but she gave up work when Alice was born. It's lovely having them so near. I see Alice often, and Thea and I are really good friends."

"You're very lucky," Janet said wistfully.

"What about your son? Is he married? What does he do?"

"He runs a small restaurant and, no, he's not married yet."

"Oh, well, there's plenty of time. Boys always seem to marry later than girls. How exciting about the restaurant. Whereabouts is it?"

"In Bristol. Stoke Bishop."

"It must be very hard work."

"Oh, it is, but he's making a great success of it." She spoke with some animation, quite different from when she described her daughter's life.

"And you don't have a job?" I asked.

"Oh, no." She seemed shocked that I should have considered such an idea. "No, my job is looking after Bernard — that's what he always says, and that's a full-time job!" Again the nervous laugh. "Of course, before I married I was a secretary — actually. I was the school secretary at Bernard's old school; that's how we met. But I gave up my job when we were married."

"To look after Bernard?"

"That's right. Though, of course, his mother was alive then. She was something of an invalid and needed a lot of care."

"I see." And I did see. Bernard seizing the opportunity to secure a slave for himself and a nurse for his mother. "Do you have any family?"

"No, both my parents died when I was quite young, and I was an only child."

Poor Janet, a perfect victim, ready to hand.

"Of course, I did do some secretarial work for Bernard at home, especially after he got his headship. There were a lot of things that he preferred not to give to the school secretary."

"Yes, I suppose there were."

"I'm afraid I haven't got very good computer skills — Bernard gets quite impatient with me sometimes. He says I must go on a course, and I suppose I will have to, but I do dread it, trying to manage new things, and all the others will be so young and able to cope."

"I'm sure you could cope too," I said, trying to put back just a little of the self-confidence that Bernard had obviously destroyed. "And I expect there'll be people of all ages."

Tris, who'd been asleep in his basket in

the kitchen and had woken up and found he was missing something, came bustling into the sitting room. He saw Foss sitting smugly on Janet's lap and trotted over and sat by her feet. She leaned over carefully and stroked him.

"He's lovely. You are lucky," she said again.

I smiled. "They're great company," I said. "You can't be lonely with two demanding animals."

We chatted for a while about general things, and I was surprised at how easy she was when not overshadowed by her horrible husband. It was plain that she had more or less sunk her own personality (whatever it might have been originally) into the sort of subservient shadow he demanded.

The sound of the wind suddenly howling down the chimney startled Tris, who leapt to his feet and began to bark. Janet looked at her watch and said, "Goodness, is that the time? I must be getting back. Bernard will be wondering what's become of me."

"Oh, don't go yet," I said. "It's only half past nine. Have another cup of tea or something."

Janet shook her head. "No, it's very kind of you, but I mustn't, really."

She lifted Foss carefully and, getting up, put him in the chair she had vacated, giving him a farewell stroke. "Thank you for a lovely evening," she said. "It's been so nice talking to you and seeing the animals. Such a lovely change . . ."

She really seemed to have enjoyed herself and I felt a wave of pity for someone who had been deprived of such simple pleasures.

"I wonder," she said hesitantly; "I wonder if I might ring for a taxi?"

"Well, of course," I said in some surprise. "I hadn't realized — I thought you'd come by car."

She shook her head. "Bernard doesn't like me driving the car," she said; then, seeing my expression, she added, "Not at night."

"There's no need for a taxi, though," I said. "I'll take you back."

"Oh, no," she protested. "I couldn't put you out like that, especially on such a terrible night!"

"It's no bother. Just hang on a minute while I change my shoes and get my coat."

It was certainly a wretched night. The rain was very heavy and although the wind had dropped a little, there was still enough to drive the rain slantwise across the road, making driving unpleasant. Janet, sitting beside me, was silent, and I was too busy to talk, having to concentrate on peering through the rain and murk dazzled by the refracted light of the headlights of the oncoming cars. The road — it was really a lane — leading to the cottage was very narrow, and I prayed that we wouldn't meet any other vehicle since I knew I'd find it almost impossible to reverse in these circumstances.

I was relieved to see the lights of the cottage shining out in the darkness, but as I pulled up onto the grass verge beside the gate, I realized that there was so much light because the front door was open.

"What on earth's happening?" I exclaimed as I got out of the car. "Whyever is the door open on a night like this?"

Janet got out more slowly. "I don't know," she said nervously. She seemed disinclined to move towards the house.

"Well, come along, then," I said rather sharply. "We're getting soaked out here."

The front door was not fully open but half ajar, almost as if the wind had blown it open. I went inside into the little hall and Janet followed me. I shut the door carefully behind us.

"Hello," I called out. "Bernard, are you there?"

There was no reply. Instead, silence; silence that had an almost positive quality in spite of the sounds of the wind and rain outside. There were two doors leading into the hall. The door of what I took to be the sitting room was on the left. It too was half open, so I went in. As well as the main wall lights, a lamp on the table was also lit. A glowing coal–effect electric fire was also on, giving the room a cozy air. On one side of the fireplace was a low-backed armchair. Because the back was low, I could see the head of the person sitting in it. For a moment I didn't really take in what I was seeing; then I heard Janet beside me cry out and I realized that she too had seen that the person in the armchair had been struck over the head and was not moving, not even at the sound of Janet's cry.

I moved slowly forward and forced myself to look more closely. Bernard was slumped in the chair, his head lolling backward. He was obviously dead. I made myself touch the side of his neck as I'd been taught in first aid, but there was no pulse. The blow to the head must have been quite severe, though there was not a lot of blood. I found that I was trembling and I felt very sick, but I knew that I had to pull myself together. I clasped my hands tightly together and, making a great effort, I turned to Janet, who was standing very still just inside the door.

"I'm so sorry," I said gently. "I'm afraid

there's nothing we can do. He's dead."

She stayed there in the doorway, putting out her hand to the doorframe as if for support. She was deathly pale and I was afraid she was going to faint, so I went towards her. But she just stood there, her lips moving though no sound came from them. I put my arm round her shoulder.

"Is there anywhere else we can go so that you can sit down?" I asked.

She made a feeble gesture to the other door leading off the hall and I led her into the kitchen. It was quite a large room, furnished as a typical farmhouse kitchen, which is what summer visitors like. There was a large pine table in the middle of the room with four chairs round it. I helped her into one of the chairs and she sat as still as a statue, her face completely blank. I became aware that the kitchen was very cold and, looking around, I saw that the glass panel of the back door had been smashed and that that door too was open.

"Burglars!" I said, and for one horrible moment I thought that the person who had done all this might still be in the house, but then I remembered the open front door and told myself that whoever it was would have gone.

Janet had made no response, and I went

over to the sink and poured her a glass of water. It seemed a feeble enough gesture but it appeared to revive her a little.

"Is he — is he really . . . ? Should we phone an ambulance?"

"I'm afraid he is dead — though I'll call an ambulance if you think we should."

"I don't know . . . I don't know. What should we do?"

"I think we ought to call the police."

"The police?" She sounded bewildered.

"They should be told as soon as possible."

"Yes. I suppose . . ."

She made no move and sat still and silent.

"Would you like me to do it?"

"Do it?" she repeated.

"Phone the police."

"Please."

"I suppose there's a phone in the other room?" I asked and moved towards the door. "Though I suppose," I said, "I ought not to touch anything. I'll use my mobile." I took it out of my bag and dialed. "Oh, bother," I said. "I can't get a signal in here. I'll have to go outside."

Janet looked at me with something like panic. "Don't leave me," she said. "Please don't leave me."

"I won't be a minute," I said soothingly. "You stay here and don't touch anything."

She shuddered. "No," she said. "I won't touch anything."

I went back through the hall and out the front door. The wind had dropped and the rain was now only a slight drizzle. I had to go up the path as far as the road before I got a signal.

When I'd made the call I went back into the house. Janet was sitting at the kitchen table just as I'd left her. She was obviously still in shock.

"They said there's a police car in the area," I said reassuringly. "They won't be long."

She nodded but didn't say anything.

"I'm so very, sorry Janet," I said. "It's a terrible thing to have happened, and it's been an awful shock for you, I know. You've been very brave."

"No," she said. "I just can't believe . . ."

"Look," I said. "I know about not touching anything, but I'm going to make you a cup of tea — you really need something stronger than water!"

There was water in the electric kettle and I found a packet of chamomile tea bags. We sat in silence listening to the sound of the kettle boiling and waiting for the police to arrive.

CHAPTER SIX

After what seemed like a very long time, we heard the sound of a car drawing up outside and a loud knock on the front door. I looked at Janet, but she shook her head so I went to open it. Two policemen stood on the doorstep.

"Sergeant Harris and Police Constable Fraser," one of them said, holding up his warrant card.

To my relief I knew one of the policemen.

"Hello, Bob," I said. "Thank goodness you're here."

We stood crowded in the hall, but I didn't feel like going back into the sitting room. I opened the door and said, "He's in there. His wife and I came in and found him like that. She's in the kitchen — as you can imagine, she's very upset." I pushed the door a little farther open. "We didn't touch anything," I said.

I moved aside to let them into the room

and went back into the kitchen. Janet was still sitting motionless at the table, but I was glad to see that she wasn't looking so ill.

"The police are here," I said, "and fortunately I know one of them — Bob Harris. I've known him since he was a child. His father used to do some gardening for me when *he* retired from the police force."

She nodded briefly but didn't say anything, and, since there didn't seem anything that I could usefully say, we sat in silence until there was a knock on the kitchen door and the two of them came in.

Bob Harris addressed Janet. "Well, now, Mrs. . . . ?"

"This is Mrs. Prior," I said since Janet appeared unable to answer, "the wife of. . . . He is — was — a sort of cousin of mine."

"And what time did you arrive back here, Mrs. Prior?" Bob asked.

Janet shook her head and looked appealingly at me. "I don't know — after half past nine, wasn't it, Sheila? You said it was half past when we left, didn't you? I'm sorry . . ." her voice trailed away.

Bob Harris, obviously deciding that he wasn't going to get anything coherent from her at the moment, turned to me.

"You got here when?"

"About a quarter to ten. Mrs. Prior had

been spending the evening with me, so I gave her a lift home. The front door was open when we got here and, as you see, the back door had been broken into."

Bob Harris went over and examined the door. "Glass panel broken and key turned from the inside." The police constable noted down the details in his notebook. "You didn't see or hear anybody in the house?"

"Well, no. I suppose we should have looked — there might have been someone upstairs, but, quite honestly, we were both too shocked and too frightened to go and look. Besides, when I saw the back door like this and finding the front door open, I assumed that whoever it was — a burglar, I suppose — had got away."

"Was anything missing?"

"I don't know. We neither of us felt much like staying in that room . . ."

"Very understandable. We'll have to go into all that later, when Mrs. Prior feels up to it. Meanwhile, madam," he continued, turning to Janet, "perhaps you could tell me what time you left here."

She seemed to have collected herself a little, and though her voice was still a little shaky she answered quite calmly. "It was about seven o'clock. I was due at Mrs. Malory's at eight, but Bernard asked me to get him some indigestion tablets — he'd had indigestion this afternoon. I said the chemist's would be shut but he said I could get some from the supermarket. I rang for a taxi and went to the supermarket first — the taxi driver waited while I went in and got the tablets. Then I went on to Mrs. Malory's. I didn't mean to stay so long, but we were having such a nice chat that I didn't notice the time. It was about half past nine when we left. I was a bit concerned that my husband would be worried because I was late coming back, but . . ." Her voice broke.

"That's very helpful," Bob was saying when there was another knock at the front door. The constable went to answer it and then, coming back, put his head round the door and said "It's SOCO, Bob. They're getting on with things."

I caught a glimpse of white-clad figures passing through the hall and sounds of activity in the sitting room. Bob Harris looked inquiringly at me.

"If both you ladies are up to it, perhaps we could just go and see if anything is missing."

"Yes," I said with a briskness I was far from feeling, "of course we'll come."

Janet got slowly to her feet and followed me to the door. We all trooped upstairs, but there was nothing out of the ordinary to be seen there. The two bedrooms, furnished for summer letting, were impersonal; only a very few objects — suitcases, toiletry bags, a few clothes hanging behind one of the doors — indicated that the cottage was inhabited. In the bathroom a glass half full of water and a towel, fallen from the rail onto the floor, were the only signs of occupation. Automatically, I leaned over and picked up the towel, putting it back onto the rail. Bob Harris turned to Janet.

"Nothing unusual here?" he asked.

She shook her head and we all went downstairs again. In the hall he said, "We really need to check the sitting room. Will you be all right?"

Janet nodded and we went in. It wasn't so dreadful, after all, because there was so much activity going on, other figures moving about their several tasks, occasionally making low-voiced remarks to one another, so that one's eyes were not focused on the silent, unmoving figure in the chair.

"Can you see if anything is missing or out of place?" Bob asked.

Janet looked round the room, bewildered and, for a while, silent. Then she said, "Not that I can see . . ."

She stood still, passive as ever, waiting, as

she must have done for many years, for someone to tell her what to do next.

"If there's nothing else?" I said and led her back into the kitchen.

"I expect Bob Harris would like us both to make a proper statement," I said. "Do you feel like doing it now, or would you rather wait and go down and do it at the police station tomorrow?"

She shook her head. "I don't mind — it doesn't matter — now, if you like."

"If you're sure."

I went back into the sitting room. "Would you like to take our statements now?" I asked Bob. "I'd really like to get her out of here."

"Well, if you think she's up to it."

He and the constable followed me into the kitchen and took our proper statements. Janet was calmer now and less confused.

"Right, then," I said to Bob. "If it's all right, I'm going to take Mrs. Prior back with me."

Janet looked up. "Oh, no, that would be an imposition — I couldn't . . ."

"Nonsense," I said. "You can't possibly stay here. Come along, you must be absolutely exhausted. Can you manage to go up and put a few things into an overnight bag?"

Janet nodded and, escorted by the constable, went slowly upstairs. They were down quite soon, the constable carrying the bag.

"We'll be off, then," I said. "You know where we are, Bob, if you want us."

The rain had stopped altogether now, but the wind had got up again and was making a melancholy noise in the trees. In the car neither of us spoke. I suddenly felt very cold, and when I turned the heater up full blast Janet murmured, "Thank you."

When we got back home we were greeted by the animals, eager to know what was causing the change in their usual routine. They followed us into the sitting room, where I put Janet into a chair, and then I went up to check the spare room. Mercifully I always keep the spare bed made up — I don't think I'd have had the strength to look out bedding and all the rest of it. I turned on the electric blanket and the heater, feeling that the least I could do was provide physical comfort for Janet. When I went down, she was sitting stroking Foss, her face quite blank.

"Are you all right?" I asked, picking up her bag. "Would you like a hot drink? I'm making one for myself."

She shook her head. "No, really — you've been so kind . . ."

As I was settling her in her room she suddenly said, "Sheila, do you think it *was* a burglary? I mean, nothing was stolen . . ."

"I really don't know," I said, "but try not to think too much about it all. You've had a tremendous shock — it's been a dreadful time for you. It's so awful about Bernard — you've been very brave. But what you need now is to get some rest. If you need anything in the night, I'm just across the landing. Don't hesitate. Stay in bed as long as you can in the morning. Good night."

Downstairs the animals reminded me that it was way past their bedtime and they hadn't been fed. As I spooned the food into their dishes it suddenly occurred to me that Janet hadn't once referred directly to Bernard and hadn't shed a single tear. As I went up to bed I glanced at the grandfather clock in the hall and saw that it was quarter past one. Strangely enough, though, I didn't feel tired, and when I finally got into bed, I didn't sleep but spent a restless night, turning over in my mind fragments of the events of the night.

The tiredness caught up with me the next morning as I dragged myself around the kitchen, feeding the animals and turning them out of doors (they weren't too keen since the wind was quite strong), and putting on the coffee. I'd just poured myself a cup and taken one reviving sip when Janet appeared in the doorway.

"Come and sit down," I said. "Did you manage to get any sleep?"

"Yes," she said, "I was very comfortable. Thank you very much."

In fact she looked much better — certainly better than I felt.

"That's splendid. What would you like for breakfast? I'll make you some herbal tea, shall I? And some toast?"

"Toast would be lovely, thank you. But do you think I might have a cup of that coffee? It smells so good."

"Of course." I poured her a cup and she drank it eagerly.

As we ate our toast I said, "What do you need to do? I imagine you want to get in touch with Christine and Luke. They'll want to come down, I'm sure, and help you with things — though, of course, anything I can do . . ."

"Yes, I will ring them, but I don't know if they can manage to come down here."

"But, surely at a time like this!"

"Well, you see, Luke won't be able to leave the restaurant — there's only him and his partner to run everything."

"What about Christine?"

Janet looked shocked. "Oh, no. I couldn't ask her; she's far too busy. No, I'm sure I can manage. But I will ring them both after breakfast."

I left her in the sitting room to make the calls and was washing up in the kitchen when she came to find me.

"They're both coming," she said. "Luke can only manage to get down here for the day, but Christine says she's going to stay." She sounded more dismayed than pleased at this prospect.

"She's very welcome to stay here," I said. "There's plenty of room."

"Oh, that is kind of you, Sheila, but we'll be all right at the cottage."

"Are you sure? It's bound to be very distressing for you. And I don't know if the police will have finished there. I suppose we ought to go and see sometime."

"Christine won't be coming till this evening, but — I hope you don't mind — I told Luke to come here."

"No, of course not. When do you expect him?"

"He said he'd be leaving right away, so it should be in a few hours."

I emptied away the washing-up water and dried my hands. "Janet," I said, "I really am most terribly sorry about Bernard — the whole thing is so awful for you and for the children. How did they take it when you rang?"

"They were upset, of course," she said, "since it was so sudden and . . ." Her voice died away.

"Were they very close?" I asked.

She seemed to consider the question for a moment, and then she said, "Christine was always his favorite, but since she's been married she hasn't seen a lot of either of us, really. Yes, she'll be upset."

"And Luke?"

"They didn't get on."

"I see." I paused to give her an opportunity to elaborate on this, but she didn't and I felt I couldn't press her. I wanted to ask whether *she* was upset, but that would have been an impertinence. "Shall we go out to lunch?" I asked, changing the subject. "I'd feel a little nervous cooking for a professional chef!"

She smiled. "Oh, goodness, Luke isn't like that at all. A sandwich would be fine if that isn't too much trouble."

"No, of course not. I've got a few things to do. You try and rest a bit — there'll be a lot to do later. Would you like today's paper?"

I left her in the sitting room seemingly

quite calm, reading the paper. I finished tidying up in the kitchen and checked the fridge to see that I had some ham for making sandwiches as well as the greater part of a Dundee cake. I let the animals in and they made straight for the sitting room, but I didn't stop them, feeling that their presence might somehow be a comfort to Janet. When I went upstairs, the door of the spare room was open and I saw that she'd stripped her bed, leaving the sheets and pillowcases neatly folded. Her overnight bag was all packed and ready to go, so she must have decided as soon as she got up that she was going back to the cottage.

This calmness and control continued to bother me. Last night she had been stunned and nervous, passive, as I had seen her when she was with Bernard — that was only natural. What wasn't natural, or so it seemed to me, was her total lack of emotion now. I could imagine that her married life hadn't been particularly happy, but surely she must have felt *something* when her husband had just died a violent death. But there seemed to be no way I could talk to her about it, no way I could get her to talk to me. I just hoped that when Luke and Christine came she'd be able to let go a little.

I made some coffee and took it into the

sitting room. She was sitting apparently quite relaxed, the paper put to one side, stroking Foss, with Tris sitting once more at her feet. She looked up when I came in.

"I thought you might like some coffee," I said.

"That would be lovely, thank you."

"So Luke and Christine both live in Bristol, then?" I asked.

"Yes — well, Christine and Jonathan live the other side of the city from Luke. He has a flat over the restaurant."

"Still, I expect they manage to see each other — and you too — quite a bit."

"They don't get on."

Again that simple statement, not elaborated, so I felt I couldn't pursue the subject.

"Running a restaurant is very hard work," I said, handing her her coffee.

"Oh, yes, it's dreadfully hard, but Luke never minds hard work, especially when it's something he's really keen on." She was suddenly animated. "And he's made such a success of it. They're doing really well. They've had several notices in magazines from food writers, and the bookings are well up on last year. It's in Stoke Bishop, quite near to Clifton — that's really where they'd like to move to, but, of course, that is the really fashionable area so the rents are dreadfully high."

"You must be very proud of him."

"Oh, yes, he's done wonderfully well."

"Luke must be a really good chef. Where did he do his training?"

"He went abroad straight after he left school. He worked a lot in France. His partner is French."

"Oh, well," I said, laughing, "we must expect him to get his first Michelin star quite soon."

We chatted for a while about the difficulties of the catering trade and other related topics, and when we'd finished our coffee I went back into the kitchen to make the sandwiches. It was fascinating to see how Janet had opened up when talking about her son, and I was curious to see what he was like. I'd just finished laying the tray (best china, cutlery and table napkins — I felt I had to make a special effort) when the doorbell rang. I opened the door to find a tall young man, dressed in motorcycling leathers and holding a crash helmet.

"Hello," he said, and his voice was particularly soft and pleasing. "I'm Luke."

CHAPTER SEVEN

He was so very much not what I'd expected that for a moment I simply stood there; then, collecting myself, I said, "I'm glad you were able to come. Your mother will be so glad to see you. Do come in; she's in the sitting room."

Janet got up when she saw him and went over and put her arms around him. I saw that at last she was crying.

"It's all right, Mum," he said. "Everything's going to be all right."

After a little while she pulled herself together and patted his shoulder. "I suppose," she said, "this outfit means you came on that dangerous motorbike. And you got here so quickly, so you must have driven far too fast."

Her voice when she was speaking to Luke was quite different from her usual diffident tones, more warm and maternal; confident, almost.

He laughed. "A hundred miles an hour and bending into all the corners"

She smiled fondly. "I wouldn't be surprised," she said. "But do take that dreadful jacket off or Mrs. Malory will think you're a Hells Angel or something."

"Oh, I'm used to motorbikes," I said. "Michael used to have one and I never had a moment's peace when he was out on it. Anyway, do sit down, Luke. I'll leave you both to talk while I see to lunch."

As I was putting out some juice and making the coffee I considered Luke. The leather gear, and the large, fancy motorbike in the drive, seemed at odds with his delicate features, his light brown floppy hair and, especially, his soft, mellifluous voice with its faintly ironic overtone, but then the most unlikely people had motorbikes. It was just a surprise; that was all.

I took my time getting the lunch together. I wanted to give Janet time to have a proper talk with her son. It had been a relief to see her finally give way to tears after her long period of unnatural calm. But when I finally went in they were sitting in silence, side by side on the sofa.

"Right, then," I said brightly, "here we are. Just sandwiches."

Luke got to his feet and took the tray,

while I went out to get the coffee and juice. When I got back I saw that he'd distributed the plates, cutlery and napkins and was already offering his mother a sandwich. He caught my faint look of surprise and said, "Sorry — do forgive me! Whenever I see food I automatically hand it around — force of habit, I suppose."

I laughed. "No, it's splendid. Thank you so much."

"Delicious ham," he said, biting into his sandwich.

"It's from the local farmers' market."

"Of course. They are wonderful, aren't they, a *great* blessing. I always try to use local produce in the restaurant; it's one of the things we've built our reputation on."

"I gather you're doing very well."

"Yes, we've managed to get a regular clientele — a neighborhood restaurant, as they say in the glossies, but that's the best sort to have in some ways, especially in the provinces. Our main trouble now is lack of space; we really do need larger premises, but the rents and rates in the best places are prohibitive."

"I can imagine."

The general conversation continued while we ate our lunch ("*Wonderful* Dundee cake! Did you make it?") and I began to wonder,

Why are we talking like this when a man is dead? Surely someone should have said something by now! As I poured the coffee I said, "I'm so very sorry about your father, Luke. It must have been a dreadful shock."

"Yes," he said, as though considering the question, "it was."

I tried again. "I don't quite know what the procedure is — I mean, I don't know if the police have finished . . . whatever they have to do at the cottage." I turned to Janet. "Would you like me to drive you both over there so that you can see what the situation is?"

She looked at Luke, who said, "I'm afraid I have to be getting back fairly soon — I just came down to see how Mum is."

"He can't leave the restaurant, you see," Janet said. "They have bookings for tonight and there's only him and Yves."

"I see."

Luke caught the faint note of disapproval in my reply and said, "I know it sounds awfully unfeeling and, honestly, I'd stay if I could, but Mum says Christine is coming and she's bound to want to make all the arrangements — I'd only be in the way."

"Christine is very efficient," Janet said.

Luke smiled. "That's one way of putting it. But bossy people come into their own at times like this, don't they?"

I started to gather up the lunch things and Luke took one of the trays and followed me out into the kitchen.

"How's she been?" he asked abruptly.

I shook my head. "I honestly don't know. Poor Janet. It was a terrible shock, as you can imagine, finding your father like that — dreadful. She was, well — stunned, I suppose. She hardly said anything. She managed to give a statement to the police. That wasn't too bad because I knew the sergeant and he was very gentle with her, and she was still in a sort of daze when we got back here and went to bed. But this morning —" I stopped.

"This morning?" Luke asked.

"So calm and matter-of-fact about arrangements, about going back to the cottage — I really don't understand it. She's never mentioned your father once, hadn't shed a tear until you came. It's as though she's on autopilot, if you know what I mean."

He nodded. "That's quite a good way of putting it, actually. She's never been allowed to be herself, to take control of her own life. If you've seen her with my father you'll know what I mean."

"Yes, I see. But no emotion —"

"There was no emotion in their marriage," Luke said, his voice hardening, "except fear on her part. So there's no reason why there should be any emotion now he has gone."

"I see," I repeated, though I didn't, quite.

Luke had now moved over to the sink and was quietly and efficiently washing up the lunch things. I went over to dry them, and the sort of intimacy that this shared task engenders allowed me to ask, "Were you fond of your father?"

He paused for a moment, apparently concentrating on rinsing a glass; then he said, "When I was a little boy I wanted so much to have his approval. I was the boy, you see, and a great deal was expected of me. I was reasonably bright academically and that pleased him, but he wanted me to be more what he called 'manly.' But I was no good at sport and outdoor things, and I never stood up for myself when I was picked on at school for being the son of one of the masters. He didn't like that. We managed to keep some sort of rapport until I left school. That's when I told him I was gay."

He tipped away the washing-up water and took some time to wring out the dishcloth and drape it neatly over the bowl.

"He didn't believe me at first — said it was only a phase, all the usual things. But, just for once, for the first time in my life, I stood up to him and told him that he had to accept it."

"That was very brave of you," I said.

He smiled sadly. "The only really brave thing I've ever done in my life."

"So what happened then?"

"He really lost it — raved and roared — 'No son of mine'; all that. Then he told me to get out and never come back. He said I was to go straightaway. I asked if I could wait until Mum came back — she'd gone up to London to check some stuff for my father in the British Library — but he said no, I had to go at once and I was never to see her again."

"Oh, no!"

He shrugged. "That's the way he was. When Mum came back, he told her she must never see me or get in touch with me ever again."

"For heaven's sake! So where did you go?"

"I had this good school friend, David — he was just a friend, nothing more — and his parents had been very kind to me. I think they knew I wasn't happy at home, though I'd never actually said anything. I went to them. I told them everything that had happened and they were marvelous. They let me stay with them, and Mr. Samuels, David's father, gave me a job in his office — just to tide me over, he said."

"What about your mother?"

"Mrs. Samuels managed to see her when my father wasn't around, and told her where I was and that I was all right."

"Poor Janet."

"It was horrible. We met secretly sometimes when we could, but she was terrified that he would find out."

"Why didn't she leave him?"

He shook his head sadly. "She had nowhere else to go and, besides, he'd sapped her will so much. . . ." He was silent for a while; then he went on. "That summer the Samuelses went on holiday in France. There was this *gîte* they always rented in Normandy, and they took me with them. It was wonderful; it changed my life."

"Hadn't you been abroad before?"

"A 'cultural tour' with my parents with my father setting me a portion of the relevant guide book to be learned by heart before we visited each monument or museum. *Not* exactly inspiring. But this was different, living in the proper country with real people, the relaxed way of life, the food! That's when I realized what I wanted to do."

"How splendid."

"The Samuelses had been going for years

to this particular restaurant, and Mr. Samuels asked if they would take me on. My French wasn't very good, but I managed to make Monsieur Picard understand how much I wanted to learn from him, so he agreed. I did all the menial jobs, worked from seven in the morning till late at night, and fell into bed exhausted in the little attic up above the restaurant, all for virtually no money. But he was a wonderful chef and he taught me well. When he thought I was good enough, he passed me on to a friend of his who had a well-known restaurant in Paris. I was so lucky."

"Hard work!"

"Yes, but it was work I loved. I was there for about six months; then I began to worry about Mum. I'd kept in touch with her through the Samuelses and she wrote to me when she could, but although she always said that everything was all right, I felt it wasn't and — well, I thought I should be near at hand. Anyway, I really wanted to see her."

"Of course."

"I came back and got a job in Bristol — sous chef in a really good restaurant in Clifton. That's where I met Yves — he was the maître d' there. He'd come over here to get more experience, but he was very homesick and we talked a lot about Paris, which is where he'd come from. Then after a bit we moved in together — he's a very special person; I've been so lucky to find him. Well, we always had this dream of starting our own place, and then, about a year ago, Yves's uncle died and left him some money — not a vast amount, but enough to start up on our own."

"That must have been very exciting."

"Oh, yes, it was wonderful, but very hard work — there's just the two of us. I do the cooking and the marketing, but Yves does the waiting, the accounts and all that sort of thing — he's *so* organized!"

"And you were able to see your mother."

"Very occasionally. But she was terrified my father would find out."

"It must have been awful for both of you. What about your sister, though?"

He gave a short laugh. "Oh, she was on my father's side. Well, she didn't actually disown me — she didn't care about my being gay. But she just thought I was — what was it she called me? — 'a pathetic little wimp.' She was the eldest, you see, and she was resentful about the years when my father concentrated on me because I was the boy."

"But didn't she care about the way he

treated your mother?"

"Oh, Christine took her cue from him; she despised Mum just as he did."

"Poor Janet."

We were both silent for a moment, and then Luke said, "I'm sorry to have gone on like this, but I wanted you to know just how it's been all these years, to understand why neither of us is sorry that he's dead."

"Yes," I said slowly, "I do understand."

Luke had been leaning against the sink while he was telling me all this, but now he straightened up and said, "Look, I've got to be going — Yves really can't cope on his own. I'm sorry to leave like this; you've been so kind. Mum was telling me how marvelous you've been. But Christine will see to any arrangements that have to be made. She's not my favorite person, as you can imagine, but she's very efficient. She'll treat Mum like a backward child, but she'll get things done and that's what matters just now. Actually," he went on, "I have been trying lately to get her on side — to look out for Mum a bit. But she's always busy and it's tiresome trying to hold any sort of conversation with an answering machine. I did have a brief word with her last night, but she had to break off in the middle to do something else — oh, well, I suppose it's not that important. I can look after Mum now."

We went back into the sitting room.

"Sorry to be so long," I said brightly, "but kind Luke's been helping me with the washing up."

Luke went over to his mother and took her hand. "I've got to go now, Mum — you know how it is."

She smiled at him. "Yes, of course, darling — you mustn't be late back."

She got up and he gave her a hug, saying, "It's all right — everything's going to be all right now."

We stood in the drive while he put his helmet on.

"That's a very fine bike," I said, looking at the gleaming red monster.

"It's a Laverda," he said. "Italian — a wicked extravagance, but Yves rides it too and it's cheaper to run than a car. And yes, Mum, I'll be careful."

He pulled down the visor of his helmet, mounted his bike, and roared off down the drive.

Janet and I went back slowly into the house.

"I hope he'll be all right," Janet said. "I do worry about that bike, especially on the motorway."

I thought how good it was to hear her talking like a normal worried mother and not just a shadowy echo of her horrible husband.

"Michael always said that bikes are safer on the motorway than on our winding lanes," I said. "I'm sure he'll be fine. What a nice boy he is! We had a chat while we were washing up and he told me how things had been for him — I think he's marvelous."

She gave me a grateful smile. "I'm so glad you like him," she said. "Especially now you know all about him. Even now, some people . . ."

"Oh, for goodness' sake," I said impatiently. "In this day and age! He's a really marvelous person, to have done what he's done with no real help from anyone, and so kind and caring. You must be very proud of him."

"Oh, I am — you can't imagine!"

"It must have been very hard for you, all those years, not seeing him."

"It broke my heart."

"But, Janet," I began awkwardly, "if Bernard was so terrible, why didn't you leave him? You were obviously a good school secretary; you could have got a job."

She shook her head. "I can't explain," she said. "I knew logically that it would be possible — Christine was grown up, at university; she'd be all right. And, anyway, she was her father's favorite — but I just couldn't. Partly, I suppose because Bernard had undermined my confidence — I didn't quite believe that I *could* do anything on my own."

"Nonsense!"

She smiled sadly. "True, though. But the other thing was, I knew he'd come after me and find me and make me go back to him. Not for love — I don't believe he ever felt that for me — but I knew that he couldn't bear to think that one of his possessions had got away from him."

"Possessions?"

"Perhaps that's not quite the right word — I don't know, though. What's that word they used to use? Chattels; that's it. I was one of his chattels, part of the furnishings, but *his,* belonging to him."

"That's terrible!"

"It was," she said simply. The clock struck the half hour and she got to her feet. "Is that the time? I have to go. I mustn't keep Christine waiting." The old, anxious note was back in her voice. "Do you mind if I ring for a taxi?"

"Don't be silly — I'll take you. But, look, if the police haven't finished at the cottage, you must both come back here. I insist."

"That's very kind of you — we'll see what Christine says."

I was sad to hear the old dull, indecisive tone and, as I got ready to go out, I wondered whether Janet was going to exchange one sort of tyranny for another.

CHAPTER EIGHT

When we got to the cottage, the constable was just taking down the crime-scene tape. As we went up the path, Bob Harris came out of the front door.

"Is it all right for us to go in now?" I asked. "Mrs. Prior's daughter is coming to stay with her for a few days — to help with arrangements and so forth."

"Yes, that's fine, Mrs. Malory. They've finished in there." He turned to Janet. "You'll need to get that smashed glass replaced in the kitchen, but everything else is all right."

"It's all right," I said, as Janet gave me a helpless look. "I'll phone Taviscombe Glass; they'll send someone out."

"Chief Inspector Eliot was saying that he'd like a word with you both sometime soon," Bob said to me. "We're dealing with it here in Taviscombe, but he's taking an interest, as you might say."

"Yes, of course. Janet," I said, "you go in. I'll follow you in a moment."

She went obediently indoors. Bob looked after her and shook his head.

"Poor lady, she's taking it very hard."

"Yes," I said mendaciously, "she's upset, of course. Have you had the pathology report? Do you know when he died?"

"Not yet. We'll keep you informed and about the inquest too, of course. It's always very awkward — the family want to know about arranging the funeral and so on."

"Yes. I'm glad Mrs. Prior's daughter is coming. I believe she's very efficient, so she'll be able to see to everything."

"Glad to hear it. I always say, it's good to have your family around you at a time like this. Well, I must be off. I expect the chief inspector will be in touch with you himself, since he's by way of being a friend, as you might say."

"Yes, he's married to my goddaughter and we've known each other for a long time."

"Well, that's all right, then," Bob said. "I'll be off, then."

"Good-bye. Give my regards to your father. I hope he's keeping well?"

"A bit of arthritis and he says he's getting slow, but his vegetable garden's still a picture. You should see his cauliflowers.

Perfect. Very difficult to grow, a perfect cauli is."

He waved cheerfully and went off to the waiting police car.

It was with some reluctance that I went into the cottage. Although the central heating had been left on, there was a chill (possibly more imagined than actual) and a feeling of desolation, which I suppose was only natural, given the circumstances. I felt that perhaps I shouldn't have sent Janet in on her own, but I didn't want her to be upset by talk of pathology reports and inquests. Though, as I considered it, I thought that she probably wouldn't have been. I heard sounds from the kitchen and, glad not to have to confront the sitting room for a moment, I went in to find Janet at the sink, filling the kettle.

"Thank goodness Christine isn't here yet. I was so afraid I might have been keeping her waiting. I thought a cup of tea would be a good idea; do you think so?"

"A very good idea," I said cheerfully. I looked at the broken glass in the back door. "I'd better go and phone the glass people. Do you think you could find a dustpan and brush and sweep up that glass while I'm doing it?"

"Oh, yes, of course. I can do that." She

opened the cupboard under the sink. "There's one here."

"Splendid," I said and went into the sitting room to make the phone call.

The room looked amazingly normal, given what had happened in it. The body was gone, of course, and as far as I could see, there were no bloodstains — though I must confess I didn't look too hard for those. The room was cold, though — it wasn't just my imagination — so I switched on the electric fire and the bright light of the coal effect gave the room an air of spurious cheerfulness. I put the electric light on too, and, just for a moment, I was able to pretend this was just an ordinary room where nothing extraordinary had happened.

I went over to the telephone and picked up the receiver. On an impulse I dialled 1471. The remote, recorded female voice said, "You were called yesterday at 19:15 hours; the number was 01463 704709. Please press 3 if you wish to be connected." I scribbled the number down on the back of a leaflet by the phone and put it in my pocket. Then I got through to Taviscombe Glass and arranged for them to send someone straightaway.

When I went back into the kitchen, Janet had swept up the glass and was looking in one of the cupboards.

"I'm looking for the biscuits," she said. "Christine will want something after her journey. I do hope biscuits will be enough — there isn't any cake. Bernard ate the last of the Victoria sponge yesterday; I was going to get some more today. Oh, dear!" She stopped suddenly. "Oh, dear, I *was* going to do some shopping today; there's hardly any food in the place. Christine will want something to eat this evening . . ."

"You can go out for a meal," I said. "She can hardly expect you to cook dinner here after what's happened."

"I suppose so," Janet said doubtfully, "but she's always said how inefficient I am. I mean, she's come all this way specially, when she's so busy. I really ought to have thought —"

"For goodness' sake. Of course she should come, however busy she is — look at Luke; I'm sure he's a lot busier — and anyway, it's her father who's dead so it's only right she should be here. Surely she would want to come for her own sake, as well as supporting you."

"You're probably right." Janet sounded unconvinced.

"After all," I said, "from what you've told me, she was her father's favorite. She must have been fond of him."

"I suppose so," Janet said, "but you can never tell with Christine; she's always kept her feelings to herself. Oh, I know what she thinks of me, and Luke too, but I never knew if she was really fond of Bernard or if she was just playing up to him because she was jealous of the way he concentrated so much on Luke, that is, when he was young, before — you know . . ."

"But what about her husband, Jonathan, isn't it? Surely she must have feelings for him, else she wouldn't have married him."

"You'd think so, wouldn't you, but I often wonder if she doesn't despise him too, like she does Luke and me."

"Surely not. What's he like?"

"Jonathan? Very nice, always very polite to me. He's successful in his job, they have a lovely home, all that, but it seems to me that he's under Christine's thumb all the time, doesn't have a will of his own."

"Often really strong people need people like that . . ."

"Like Bernard and me?" Janet said with a wry smile. "I don't think it's as bad as that, because he's a man and he's got a job and is out in the world, but, yes, I've seen the similarities and I've been sorry for him."

"I see."

"I know he'd have liked children," Janet went on, "but Christine wanted a career — said there was plenty of time, and I suppose there is; well, not plenty of time, but enough — but I don't think she really wants any. They'd be a distraction, you see; they'd take at least part of Jonathan's attention from her."

There was a sound of a car drawing up outside.

"Oh, that'll be the glass people," I said. "I'll go and let them in."

But when I opened the front door I saw that it was Christine. She was quite different from her brother — tall, with dark hair worn shorter than his, she obviously resembled Bernard, while Luke took after Janet, not only, I imagined, in looks.

"Mrs. Malory?" she asked, and her voice was stronger and less pleasing. "I'm Christine Taylor."

"Yes, of course, do come in. Your mother's been expecting you."

I led the way into the kitchen, where Janet was standing by the table, her eyes fixed anxiously on the door.

"Hello, dear," she said. "It was so good of you to come when I know how busy you are."

Christine took off her driving gloves,

rather in the manner of someone rolling up their sleeves to perform some difficult task.

"Right, then," she said, "you'd better tell me what's been going on."

"Well, your father — well, you know about that — all very distressing — the police have been so kind — and, of course, Sheila — it's all right to stay here, they said, that is, if you don't mind — I've given them a statement, but I think they want to talk to me again . . ."

Her voice trailed off, and Christine, who had been listening to these disjointed remarks with growing impatience, said, "Oh, for heaven's sake, Mother, pull yourself together; do *try* to be coherent." She turned to me and said, "Perhaps *you* could tell me exactly what the situation is."

"Your mother has been very upset," I said coldly, "and under a great deal of strain. Not surprisingly, given the circumstances."

She seemed a little taken aback by my manner but pulled herself together and said in a more conciliatory tone, "Yes, of course, I understand that. Still, if you could kindly give me the details."

I told her what had happened as concisely as possible, just the facts, since I didn't think she'd want to know about feelings and reactions.

"So," she said when I'd finished, "you don't have any real information about the postmortem or the inquest, so I can't make the funeral arrangements yet."

"We may know more," I said, "when we go to the police station, tomorrow, perhaps. I gather they would like to see us again."

"I can't see why that's necessary if you've already given statements. No, I think I'd better go down to the police station myself now and sort this out."

"I don't think that would be much use," I said firmly. "Chief Inspector Eliot won't be there — he's based in Taunton and he has overall control of the case. I don't think Sergeant Harris will be able to tell you anything more than I have."

For a moment I thought that she was going to go anyway, but then she turned to her mother and said, "Well, it can't be helped. It just means that I'll have to stay another day."

The doorbell rang again.

"That will be the people to fit a new pane of glass in the door," I said. "I'd better let them in. Perhaps you'd be more comfortable in the sitting room while they're doing it."

"I'll take my suitcase upstairs," Christine said; then, pausing at the door, she said to me, "Make sure you get an invoice from them — the owner of the cottage will have to pay for that. He can claim it on his insurance."

It was quite a relief after that to chat to the young man putting in the new glass.

"Bit of a mess," he said cheerfully, getting out his tools. "Burglary, was it?"

"Would you like a cup of tea?" I asked, avoiding the question. "I'm just about to make one."

The kettle that Janet had put on was still warm and didn't take long to boil. I poured a cup for the young man and put the teapot and the rest of the tea things onto a tray and took it into the sitting room. Janet got to her feet.

"Oh, dear, *I* was going to do that, wasn't I? Thank you so much, Sheila," she said vaguely.

I poured the tea for them and took my own cup back into the kitchen. I told myself that they'd want to be alone to talk things over, but, of course, really it was because I couldn't bear to listen to Christine bullying her mother.

Back in the kitchen the glass had been fitted and the young man was drinking his tea.

"You've been quick," I said.

"Straightforward job," he said. "No problem." He put down his cup. "Thanks for the tea. I've left the invoice on the table — it's a holiday cottage, isn't it, so you'll be wanting to send that to the landlord. Cheerio."

As I saw him out I considered how much less irritating that information was coming from him than from Christine. I went back into the kitchen and took my time drinking my own cup of tea and washing up the two cups. When I could spin these tasks out no longer I went back reluctantly into the sitting room.

"Well, now," I said brightly, "is there anything I can do?"

"There's not much anyone can do," Christine said, "until we get more information."

"No," I said, "I can see it's difficult for you."

"I'll just go and see if the bed's made up in the other bedroom," Janet said, "and if the heating's on."

She got up and went out of the room quickly, as though escaping, which I suppose she was. I sat down on the sofa — I noticed that neither of them had taken the chair Bernard had been found in — and said, "I'm so sorry about your father; it must be dreadful for you — the way he died . . ."

"I imagine it was a burglar," she said.

"Presumably he broke in and my father confronted him, which is what he would have done, and the man panicked and hit him over the head."

"That's what it looks like," I agreed.

"Well, it must have been what happened," she said irritably. "It's highly unlikely anyone would have wanted to murder him."

"No, of course not," I said, "and down here too, where he didn't really know anyone."

Christine gave me a sharp glance as if picking up the ambivalence of my remark. "Exactly," she said. "I was very fond of my father," she went on. "He was always an inspiration to me. He was a fine headmaster; his school was in the top division of all the school league tables."

"How splendid," I said inadequately.

"Mother never really appreciated what a remarkable man he was," she went on, "but she was devoted to him. Indeed, I don't know how she's going to get on without him, and I'm afraid my life is very full so that I can't give her the attention she will need. I can see it's going to be quite a problem."

"Luke seems very devoted to her," I ventured. "He came down earlier today to see how she was."

"Oh, Luke," she said dismissively. "He's always fussing about her. You may have heard the story. Very unpleasant. I don't say my father was right, turning him out as he did, but he was a man with very strong principles and I can see his point of view, even if it's not one that's currently acceptable. Luke was a great disappointment to him in many ways."

"He seems to have made a success of his restaurant," I said.

"Oh, cooking — that's hardly a proper career, is it?"

"A lot of people think so nowadays," I said.

"Anyway, I knew that Mother had been seeing him. Of course I didn't tell Father; he would have been very upset and, although I didn't approve of the deceit, I didn't see any real harm in it. The only thing was Luke kept ringing me up, asking me if she was all right — very tiresome. Actually, he rang me yesterday evening; most inconvenient."

"He rang you last night?"

"Yes, about eight o'clock; well, it was just before eight because there was a television program that I wanted to see — an important documentary about global warming — that started at eight. And, of course, it was just the same old thing, asking about Mother. Not that I could hear half of what he was saying, because he was ringing from that restaurant of his and it was very noisy. So I said I didn't have time to talk and put the phone down."

"Perhaps Luke could look after your mother now," I suggested.

"Good gracious no; that would be most unsuitable, given his circumstances. Besides, it's a question of where she's going to live; obviously she can't stay in that large house all by herself. No, I suppose I'll have to try and find some sort of flat for her, though, of course, she could go into sheltered housing. I must see what the options are."

I was depressed at the thought of Christine taking over, as it were, from where Bernard had left off, and I very much hoped that Luke would encourage his mother to stand up for herself at last. Certainly she had seemed a different person when they were together, and perhaps Christine would be "too busy" to bother about taking control of her mother's life.

"I think you'll be all right in that end bedroom," Janet said to Christine as she came into the room. "It has a lovely view up over the hills," she added in a placatory tone.

"I'm sure it will be perfectly adequate," Christine said, picking up the tea tray in a brisk manner that suggested that in doing so she was taking over the reins of government. "Thank you very much, Mrs. Malory — may I call you Sheila, since we are related? You have been most kind."

When the door had closed behind her, I said to Janet, "Shall I call for you to go to the police station tomorrow?"

"Well . . ." She hesitated. "Christine said she would be going, so . . . well, perhaps not. I'll ring and let you know what happens, shall I?"

"Yes, that will be fine. Though, as I'm going there tomorrow anyway, we may meet there."

"Oh, dear," she said anxiously. "Christine might not like . . . But no, of course," she went on. "It would be perfectly natural, wouldn't it? I mean, she wouldn't think we'd arranged it, would she?"

"It'll be all right," I said, going to the door. But, having seen Christine, I had the gravest doubts that it would be.

Chapter Nine

As it happened, I didn't get to the police station the next morning. I'd fed the animals and fed myself and I'd finished the washing up when I thought I'd just defrost some prawns as a treat for Foss when I came back. So I got the pack out of the freezer, and as I was undoing it the whole thing slipped out of my hands and the contents were scattered over the floor. Putting the animals, enthusiastic to help, out of doors, I collected the prawns, having to get down on my hands and knees (no easy feat these days) to retrieve the stray prawns from under the fridge and the washing machine. Telling myself they were only for the animals, who wouldn't mind, I put most of them back in the bag, replaced it in the freezer, and left a small amount in water to defrost. I then felt obliged to mop the kitchen floor with disinfectant in case it might smell of prawns.

The whole incident left me feeling disproportionately exhausted, and I was just sitting down to recover when the telephone rang. It was Anthea.

"Sheila, what do you know about this concert they're having in the Methodist Hall?"

"What do you mean?"

"Who's organizing it?" she said impatiently. "They've got that string quartet *we* always have for the concert at Brunswick Lodge for the restoration appeal."

"I haven't the faintest idea. Doesn't it say on the poster?"

"There isn't a poster, just a notice in this week's *Free Press* — surely you've seen it."

"Well, actually, as it happens, I haven't had time to look at the *Free Press.*"

Anthea, who always reads the paper from cover to cover the minute it comes out every Friday, gave an exclamation of surprise and disbelief. "Well, anyway," she continued, "I'd very much like to know who's behind it." She made it sound like a revolutionary plot. "I mean, we've *always* had that quartet, and now if these people — whoever they are — are going to use them as well for their fund-raising concerts, everyone is going to be very *confused.*"

"I don't see why they should; I mean, when they played for us it was at Brunswick Lodge. Quite different."

"Well," Anthea said, clearly unconvinced, "if you find out who these people are, let me know. Now, what I want to ask you is, can you help Monica with the coffee morning on Wednesday? Mrs. Galbraith was going to do it, but they've brought her hip replacement forward so she'll be going into hospital on Monday."

"Well . . ."

"It's only for a couple of hours; I'm sure you can manage that."

Since Fate and Anthea can never be denied, I said that yes, I'd do it.

"Oh, good. And if you should happen to be making some scones, they're always welcome."

Sighing, I went out into the kitchen to mark Wednesday's date on the calendar and let in the animals, who rushed in, anxious to see what had been going on in their enforced absence. It had been raining and they were both wet and muddy, so I had to dry them both, which they hate, thereby getting pretty muddy myself. Foss, when he escaped, immediately crouched down beside the fridge, hooked out a prawn that had escaped my notice, and began to eat it noisily. Tris, put out by this, began whining for food, so I had to get out the dry food for them both and was just putting the packets away when the doorbell rang.

As I went to answer it, I caught a glimpse of myself in the mirror in the hall, looking disheveled and with a streak of dirt down the side of my face, and hoped that my caller wasn't someone who'd think this was my normal appearance. My caller, in fact, was Roger Eliot.

"Good heavens," he said, "what *have* you been up to?"

"Come in," I said. "It's been one of those mornings!"

I led the way into the kitchen, put the kettle on, and got out the tin of chocolate digestives. I also got the kitchen towel and wiped my face vigorously.

"It's lovely to see you," I said, "but I imagine it's business and you're not just dropping in for a chat."

"I'm afraid so — though the tea and biscuits are a welcome addition."

"I suppose it's about Bernard Prior. I was coming down to the station — Bob Morris said you'd be there this morning — but, as you can see, minor domestic problems have held me up."

"It's nicer," Roger said, taking a second

biscuit, "like this."

"We did make statements — Bernard's wife, Janet, and I — the night it happened."

"Yes, I've seen those. Pretty coherent, I thought, after what must have been a horrible experience for you both."

"Well, yes, it was, but do you know, somehow, at the time it didn't seem real — I can't explain, but it didn't seem like a murder at all."

"It wasn't."

My hand shook as I was pouring the tea, splashing it into the saucer.

"But — but I was there; I *saw* him."

"You saw a dead man in a chair, but he hadn't been murdered."

"He'd been struck on the head," I said. "I saw the blood."

"Very little blood, though."

"Well, yes — I can remember thinking. —"

"That's because he was already dead when someone hit him on the head."

"Already dead?" I echoed stupidly.

"We have the forensic report. He died of a heart attack."

"No! When?"

"The times are a bit tight, but they think there was a gap of about an hour between his heart giving out and the attack by whoever it was."

"He must have died soon after Janet left," I said. "Of course! She said he'd been complaining of indigestion all afternoon; that's why she stopped off at the supermarket to get some tablets for him. What an extraordinary thing!" I got a fresh saucer and poured the tea. "But surely," I said, "the burglar would have seen that he was dead, wouldn't he?"

"Not necessarily. He was sitting in that low-backed chair, with his head back and his eyes closed. The burglar — if it was a burglar — may have thought that he was asleep."

"I suppose that's possible," I conceded.

"Though, actually, I'm not really sold on the idea that it was a burglar."

"But there was a forced entry," I said — "that smashed glass panel in the back door and the front door left open when he — the burglar, that is — panicked and ran away."

"Hmm, yes, but it all looks a bit pat, don't you think?"

"What do you mean?"

"Just what you'd expect to find if there had been a burglary — the sort of thing you see in television cop drama — all carefully set up."

"Well, yes, I see what you mean. And, of

course," I added, "nothing was taken."

"Exactly."

"But if the burglar hit Bernard over the head, not realizing he was dead, and then saw that he *was,* and thought he'd killed him, then he'd panic and run away."

"True. But I still think the whole setup is too good to be true."

"But if it isn't a burglary that went wrong, what *is* it?"

"How about attempted murder?"

"But the whole thing's bizarre!"

"That's one way of putting it."

"And really horrible," I went on, "if you come to think of it. Striking a dead person."

"But if you didn't know he was dead? Which is worse — murder or this?"

"If you put it like that, I suppose . . . But presumably if you catch whoever it was, they'd be guilty of murder, wouldn't they?"

"No."

"But what would they be guilty of?"

"In this particular case? I daresay we could have them for breaking and entering."

"And that's all!"

"In law, hitting a dead person over the head is not a criminal offense."

"Good heavens. Not even grievous bodily harm?"

"Not in this case."

I drank the rest of my tea in an effort to clear my mind.

"Does Janet know?" I asked.

"Yes. I saw her and her daughter at the station before I came to see you."

"Poor Janet. How did she take it?"

"She was very upset. I'm afraid she more or less collapsed. Her daughter took her home. Not, however, before she — the daughter, that is — favored me with several scathing comments concerning police inefficiency, with especial reference to our outdated and dilatory methods. She was particularly concerned that I couldn't give her the date of the inquest or when the body would be released. Apparently, the entire educational system of the South West has had to be put on hold until she gets back."

"There will be one, then? An inquest, I mean."

"The circumstances are unusual enough to warrant one, certainly. I imagine it will simply confirm that death was from natural causes."

I shook my head. "I just can't take it in."

"It's unusual, certainly."

"So whoever thought they'd killed Bernard doesn't know he was already dead and . . ."

"And they needn't have bothered. That's

right. It'll come as a bit of a shock when they do find out." Roger took the last biscuit. "Sorry, do you mind? I didn't have time for any breakfast."

"Of course not. Would you like some cake or something more substantial — a sandwich, perhaps?"

"No, these are fine."

"So," I said, "will you still be looking for who did it?"

"Obviously there'll be some sort of inquiry, but not top priority, like it would have been if it was murder."

"I see."

Roger brushed a few stray crumbs from his jacket. "Do you have any idea who might have wanted him dead?"

"Goodness yes!" I began. "Well, the person who had the most reason to be glad he's gone is his wife — he was an appalling bully; he ruined her life — but it can't be her because she was with me the whole time. His son had every reason to hate him too, but he was in Bristol, and so was his daughter, Christine — though she seems to have been quite fond of her father."

"Not promising."

"But Bernard was a thoroughly unpleasant person and the most terrible bore. He must have annoyed a lot of people."

"Much as one would like to, one doesn't usually kill people because they're boring," Roger said. "And down here, away from his home territory, who would have a strong enough motive?"

I shrugged. "I don't know. He had several relations round here, and I know he went to visit all of them — because of this family history thing — before he died. There may have been some dark disagreement that I don't know about. I suppose Janet might be able to tell you. Not," I added, "that he'd have been likely to tell her anything important."

"Well," Roger said, getting to his feet, "have a think, and if you come up with anything, let me know. By the way," he added, smiling, "you still have a great smear of mud on your forehead."

After he'd gone I went upstairs to tidy myself. I felt I must go and see Janet. No wonder she'd collapsed. This extraordinary piece of news — such a loathsome thing to have happened — coming on top of finding Bernard dead. She'd taken that with apparent calm, but this new revelation was enough to overset anyone.

When I got to the cottage, Christine opened the door.

"I came as soon as I heard," I said. "How's

Janet?"

"She's calmer now," Christine said, leading the way into the sitting room, "but she was quite hysterical for a while. She's lying down at the moment, so it's fortunate you came. I need to go out for a while — there's no food in the house; so inefficient. But I do feel someone should be with her, if you wouldn't mind staying till I get back."

"Of course I will," I said, surprised at Christine's comparatively conciliatory tone. "I was so sorry," I went on, "to hear of this new development. It's perfectly horrible to think of such a thing happening. It's no wonder poor Janet's so upset. And apparently there's nothing in the law to punish whoever did it."

"I shall certainly want my solicitor's ruling on *that*," Christine said. "It would be unthinkable if someone who did such a thing were to go unpunished. Right, then," she said briskly, "you can go on up; I don't think Mother is asleep."

Actually, Janet was sitting in a chair by the window. She had the same stunned look that she had had when we discovered Bernard's body. She turned as I knocked and went into the room.

"Sheila?" she said vaguely; then, obviously trying to pull herself together, "How kind of you to come."

"You must be feeling awful," I said. "Such a shock."

"Yes," she echoed, "such a shock."

"An unspeakable thing to have happened."

She was silent for a moment, and then she said, "He was dead, you see. Dead when . . ." Her face contorted and she began to cry. "Horrible," she kept repeating, "horrible . . ."

She was sobbing violently and painfully now, every vestige of her previous calm quite gone. I knelt down beside her.

"I know," I said, "it's a really dreadful thing to have happened, but you mustn't upset yourself like this; you'll make yourself ill." I spoke soothingly, as if to a child. If it had been a child, I could have said that everything would be all right, but, in spite of her childlike helplessness, Janet was not a child and I knew that everything was going to be far from all right. After a few minutes her sobs grew less and she was obviously making an effort to control herself.

"I'll go and make you a cup of tea," I said, seizing on the one thing we feel we *can* do in difficult circumstances. "That's if you're all right for a moment?"

She nodded without speaking, and I went downstairs. In a way, I was glad to see the tears; it made the whole situation seem more normal. A wife should cry for her dead husband, shouldn't she? Well, possibly not in some situations. But I could see that the unusual and unpleasant circumstances of Bernard's death might well have stirred depths of feeling that had little to do with sorrow. It occurred to me, though, that I was glad that Bernard had died a natural death and that he hadn't known of the blow someone had delivered so cruelly. I hoped Janet might feel the same. As for Christine, well, I didn't know. Surely she must have been moved by this new aspect of her father's death. The impregnable carapace of self-satisfaction might hide some real emotion, but she was certainly not going to show it to me, nor, probably, to her mother.

When I took the tea upstairs Janet seemed to have recovered — she was no longer crying, but her face wore a look of desolation that I found more upsetting than her more overt signs of grief.

"Here," I said, handing her the cup, "drink it up while it's hot."

The banal remark seemed to cheer her, and she gave me a little smile.

"Thank you, Sheila, you've been very kind. I'm so sorry I broke down like that. It's just that it was all so — so unexpected."

"I think you've been very brave," I said. "Especially now."

She shook her head but didn't say anything.

"How long is Christine staying?" I asked as I poured myself a cup, feeling that I needed a little comfort too. "Has she decided?"

"I think she's going back tomorrow — it's so difficult for everyone when she's away — but she'll be coming back as soon as they release — is that the word? — Bernard's body." She spoke the last word hesitantly as if unwilling to use it.

"Look, Janet," I said, "you can't stay here on your own. Do come back with me when Christine goes."

She smiled and shook her head. "It's really sweet of you, Sheila, and I do appreciate it, but I think I'd rather stay here."

"But —"

"You see," she went on, "I have to do things on my own now, and this will be the first thing, the first time, really, since I married Bernard that I've actually been on my own and made any sort of decision for myself. And do you know," she added, faintly surprised, it seemed to me, at what she was saying, "do you know, I'm rather looking forward to it."

Chapter Ten

The phone was ringing as I let myself into the house. It was Thea.

"Are you all right?" She asked. "You sound a bit breathless."

"I've just got in," I said. "I had to go and see Janet." I told her what had happened.

"How absolutely awful. What a vile thing to have happened!" she exclaimed.

"I must say, it did shake me a bit, and Janet really broke down."

"I should think so, poor soul. But look, Sheila, are you sure you're all right for tonight? I'm sure Virginia would quite understand if we didn't make it."

I suddenly remembered that I'd agreed to babysit Alice while Thea and Michael went out to dinner. "No, really, I'm fine," I said. "I've been looking forward to seeing Alice."

"Well, if you're sure. About seven, then.

Alice will have had her supper and her bath."

Alice greeted me with enthusiasm, heightened by the sight of the small furry toy I'd bought for her — young children always associate grandparents with such tribute items and come to expect them.

"Bunny rabbit," she said with satisfaction. "Benjamin Bunny," she added. "Gran, read me the story?" she suggested.

"You go and get the book, then, and hop into bed, and I'll come upstairs."

When Alice had gone, Michael said, "Thea will be down in a minute. She's been telling me about Bernard. Pretty grisly!"

"Roger said that in law there's nothing to be done — that's most peculiar."

"The law *is* peculiar," Michael said, "and extraordinary and, sometimes, unfair — but there you are!"

"Goodness knows," I said, "I had no time for Bernard — especially when I discovered how he treated Janet and his son, Luke, but for something like that . . ."

"I know."

"But the fact remains that someone attempted to kill him. Attempted murder, whatever the law might say."

"Or aggravated burglary," Michael suggested.

"Roger didn't seem to think so," I said, "and the more I think about it, the more I feel there was something not quite right about the whole scene. I mean, it was horrible and really upsetting, but — well — something *arranged* about it all."

"But if it was murder," Michael said, "do you have any idea who might have wanted to kill him?"

"Both Janet and Luke had every reason to want him dead," I replied, "but neither of them could have done it. No, it's a bit of a mystery."

"Oh, dear," Michael said, "my heart sinks when you use that word. Please don't tell me you intend to investigate a nonexistent murder!"

"You must admit someone ought to, and the police aren't going to give it any sort of priority."

"You could," Michael suggested, "let sleeping dogs lie — no, silly of me to suggest it. I know you can't resist giving them a little prod."

"Actually," I said, "I feel I owe it to Janet to make some sort of inquiries. She's in such a peculiar state I'm sure it would help if there was some sort of — horrid word — *closure.* It might help her to come to terms with it."

"I suppose it's as good an excuse as any for interfering," Michael said. "Just don't go poking about in any really dark corners. Where are you going to start, anyway?"

"I don't know. I'll have to have a think."

"She's in bed with her book," Thea said, coming downstairs, "but she's had a lot of exercise and fresh air today, so I think she'll be really sleepy very soon. I've left the sandwiches and things out in the kitchen — help yourself; you know where everything is."

"Probably better than we'll be eating," Michael said. "Virginia's a nice girl, but her cooking's terrible!"

Thea was right; Alice fell asleep halfway through the second reading of *Benjamin Bunny,* and as I was eating my sandwiches (chicken and stuffing — delicious), I was, indeed, trying to think who might have had a reason for killing Bernard. Motive — such a cold, impersonal word for the fierce emotion that could make someone take the life of another human being — what might be the motive? It could be something Bernard had done to someone, or else the knowledge he might have had that would be dangerous to another person. Either was a possibility. It seemed that Bernard had been capable of making other people's lives unbearable, so if he'd behaved like that to Janet and to Luke, what other lives might he have destroyed? But — I was brought up short — presumably anyone he'd injured in that way would be in Bristol and not in Taviscombe, so why kill him *here?*

I poured myself another cup of coffee as an aid to concentration. Did that mean, I wondered, that the person in question — the murderer; I must try to think of him (or her) as that — was local and Bernard was killed now because he *was* here? The only people who might have that sort of motive were members of the family, all connected in some way, however distantly, with the family tree that Bernard had been putting together. People like me. Was it possible that someone . . .

My thoughts were interrupted by the appearance of a small, forlorn figure trailing a comfort blanket behind her.

"Gran — Gran, I woke up and there's a tiger in my room and he won't go away!"

I went over and picked her up. "Good gracious," I said. "We can't have that! It's long past bedtime for all tigers."

As it turned out, I had no opportunity to do any sort of investigating for the next couple of days because I suddenly realized that I'd come up against the deadline for a review I was doing and everything had to go on hold until that was finished. Then, no sooner than that was out of the way, I had to help Monica with the coffee morning at Brunswick Lodge. I hadn't the time to make the scones that Anthea demanded, so I took a sponge out of the freezer and hoped it would be sufficiently defrosted to be edible by the time I got there.

"That's all right, Sheila," Monica said, "I'll put it up for a raffle at the end of the morning — cakes always go well — it'll be fine by then."

We were quite busy for a while, but towards the end of the morning, when most people were busily chatting to acquaintances they saw every day (the main purpose of coffee mornings), Monica said, "I was so interested in that talk your cousin — he is a cousin, isn't he? — gave here a little while ago. Such a fascinating subject! I often wish I had the time to investigate *my* family tree. There's a lot of interest in that sort of thing now, isn't there? Did you see that series on the television? Amazing the things they found out — not all of them good, of course. That's the problem, I suppose; you never know what's going to turn up. It might be something you really didn't want to know." She laughed. "Or that you didn't want other people to know, for that matter!"

"That's very true," I said.

The thought stayed with me and lingered as I made myself some lunch. It was quite possible that, in the course of his research, Bernard had come across something a member of the family didn't want known. Still, it must have been a pretty big something for someone to try to commit murder to stop it coming out. And, again, if there was something, did Bernard *know* it was important? Had he been actually blackmailing whomever it was? I felt he was capable of it — though perhaps not for money, but for power or influence, in some way, over his victim.

My thoughts were interrupted by the sight of the toaster expelling two pieces of blackened bread. Why is it that no toaster, however carefully you set it, will ever consistently produce toast that isn't either underdone or burnt? By the time I'd made more toast, heated my soup, and got out the cheese and biscuits, the animals, having long since consumed their own food, joined me, hoping to share in mine. So I decided to postpone any thoughts on the matter until after lunch, when I could look out the material Bernard had given me and see whether I could find anything that might give me some sort of clue. I gave Tris and Foss a piece of cheese each and devoted myself to my lunch and the review pages of *The Spectator.*

It was with some reluctance that I spread out the various sheets of family trees and other information that I'd stuffed into a drawer of my desk and not looked at since Bernard had left. I found that, just as when I'm faced with any sort of numbers, my mind freezes over, it was just the same with this sort of material. Naturally I could trace a family, generation by generation, straight down the line, but once I had to cross-reference it, as it were, I found it difficult to make any connection apart from the obvious one that they were all related. It was even more difficult when I tried to trace a person from one family tree to another — something Bernard seemed to delight in doing. As for the dates, well, I've never been able to get my mind round *them.*

I did try. I struggled with the wretched papers (all an inconvenient shape and size, with some pasted together) for well over an hour. Then, in despair, I turned to Bernard's notes. These appeared to be notes from parish registers and stuff from the Public Record Office — more dates again — and some census returns. I felt I was drowning in a sea of information.

"This is ridiculous," I said to Tris, who'd been patiently sitting by my feet, hoping that if he leaned his weight against me long enough, I'd remember he was there and take him for a walk. "It's all too much to take in. Not for the whole family. I must try and do it one person at a time. Make a list of who Bernard was going to see while he was down here and look them up one by one." This (I suppose) obvious idea so pleased me that I swept all the papers back into a pile and put them back into the drawer. "I'll do it tomorrow."

I was just nerving myself to face the cold wind outside and take Tris for a walk when Rosemary rang. She'd been away for a fortnight looking after an old aunt, her mother's sister, who was ill, and I'd missed her very much.

"My dear, I've only just heard — Roger told me. What a ghastly thing to have happened! It must have been a terrible shock; are you all right? Look, come on over now and have a cup of tea and tell me all about it."

"I was just going to take Tris for a walk
—"

"Bring him too. He and Alpha can have a
runabout in the garden."

I felt a lightening of spirits. Of course the
best thing of all is to have your loving family around you, but there's nothing quite
the same as a good chat with your best
friend.

"I'm so glad you're back," I said as we sat
by the kitchen window watching Tris and
Alpha, Rosemary's elderly boxer, chasing
each other sedately round the garden. "How
was Auntie Gwen?"

"Better when I left — it was quite a bad
go of bronchitis. She's a game old thing but
a terrible patient; after the first couple of
days she refused to stay in bed and I had to
keep a very beady eye on her or she'd have
been trotting around trying to look after
me!"

"It sounds as if you had your hands full."

"Oh, she's good company — she's got a
sharp tongue, just like Mother, but a kinder
nature! But it's so *cold* in Lincoln — all
those east winds — and the streets are so
steep, and you can't take the car because
parking's even worse than it is here. I was
quite worn out by the end of it. Jolly glad to
be home, as you can imagine."

"I'm sure Jack was delighted to have you back. How did he manage while you were away?"

"Well, Jilly popped in every day and left him some food and saw to Alpha, and he ate with them several evenings. That was all right, and he did *try* to keep things going here, but you know how hopeless he is about the house; it'll take me ages to get things back in order."

"Never mind; he'll really appreciate you for a bit now you're back."

Rosemary laughed. "The appreciation's starting to wear off already, and I only got back yesterday. Still, I did miss him! It made me realize how much I depend on him, just being there." She looked at me. "I can't imagine how you managed after Peter . . ."

"It takes time," I said.

The kettle made bubbling noises and Rosemary got up to make the tea.

"Anyway, what about this awful thing with your cousin? I know you weren't too keen on him, but it must have been dreadful to find him like that. And with his wife there too."

"It was. But somehow the full force of what had happened didn't really hit me. I was so busy trying to look after Janet — she was in a very vulnerable state — so I suppose I just sort of focused on her."

"Poor woman," Rosemary said sympathetically. "How did she react? I'd have been in hysterics!"

"She was stunned, very quiet, almost more difficult to deal with in a way. Later, of course, after we heard about Bernard being already dead when . . . when he was attacked, she really broke down — very painful."

"I'm not surprised; it's a really gruesome thing to have happened. So where is she now?"

"She's insisted on staying in the holiday cottage they were renting. I did try to persuade her to come and stay with me, but she wouldn't."

"Some people are better on their own when something awful's happened," Rosemary said thoughtfully. "Anyway, you've done all you can. It can't have been easy."

"It's been sort of baffling," I said. "I really couldn't make her out half the time. I mean, she's been bullied and put upon by that dreadful man all her married life, so, yes, I can see that she wouldn't actually *grieve* for him, but she seems — I can't explain it properly — she seems to be letting the whole thing flow over her. Although, as I said, she reacted, quite violently, to the fact that he'd been attacked after his death, she seems to have gone back to this passive state."

"Well, I think it's a good thing she's not staying with you," Rosemary said firmly. "I mean, I'm very sorry for her and all that, but she does sound a bit of a problem. After all, *you* had a nasty shock too, and you've been rallying round ever since. I mean, you hardly know her, so it's a bit hard that you're having to do everything. What about her family; can't they take some of the burden?"

"Her son, Luke, did come straightaway, but he could only stay for few hours. He runs a restaurant and had to get back. I think he truly wanted to stay, but it wasn't possible. Her daughter, Christine, is a teacher, quite high-powered, and she's been here for two days — she's spoken to the police and is sorting out the inquest and the funeral. But she's off tomorrow and, quite honestly, I think Janet will be glad to see the back of her — she's really a bully, like her father."

"I must say, they all sound a bit much! So how long is this Janet person staying?"

"I don't know. Until after the inquest, I suppose, and she'll have to arrange about getting the body back to Bristol for the funeral."

"Just don't let her put everything onto you. Let the family do it."

"I expect Christine will want to do all that," I said. "She's obviously the organizing type. But I've no idea how long it will be, and I really don't like to think of poor Janet alone in that cottage."

"Well, you'll do what you have to do. I know, but just don't let it get out of hand."

"I won't," I promised.

"What you need," Rosemary said, "is a diversion. You can help *me* out."

"Oh?"

"Delia's got a solo in Miss Morton's show — you know Delia's been going to her ballet classes for ages — and Jilly gave me two tickets for the Friday (they're going on the Saturday — last night and all that), and, of course, there's no way I can persuade Jack to come, so *would* you?"

"Of course, I'd love to. I didn't realize Delia was still doing ballet. I thought she was horse mad now."

"Horse *and* ballet mad," Rosemary said. "Poor Jilly spends her whole life ferrying her from one to the other. Still, she's getting quite tall now, so perhaps she'll soon be too big for ballet. It doesn't seem to matter so much for riding."

"Has she persuaded Roger and Jilly to buy her a pony yet?"

"No, they're holding out. Roger thinks he might be able to get her a loan pony — you know, you have them on loan from someone who needs them exercised and looked after for a few months. That's not so bad, though anything to do with horses is hideously expensive. Still, now she's a teenager Jilly's decided it's better the horsey set than the disco set!" She smiled. "Just you wait; you've got all this to come yet with Alice!"

"Oh, dear," I said. "It all sounds terribly exhausting."

"Families *are* exhausting," Rosemary said, "but very rewarding."

"Yes," I agreed. "Though," I added, "I suppose it depends on the family."

CHAPTER ELEVEN

When I put on my warmer coat to go out to the shops, I felt in the pocket for my scarf and found the leaflet I'd thrust in there the day after we discovered Bernard's body. What with everything else, I'd forgotten all about it. I looked at the telephone number I'd scribbled down and saw that it was local. I took off my coat and picked up the telephone. I dialed 141, so that whoever it was wouldn't know who was calling; then I rang the number. After about six rings the answering machine clicked in: "This is Brookside Farm. If you want to leave a message for Harry or Pam, please speak after the tone."

I replaced the receiver and stared at the telephone thoughtfully. Why on earth would Harry be telephoning Bernard? Pam said he found Bernard so tiresome he'd do anything to avoid him. So why? It had to be something to do with Bernard's research, but I didn't think Harry was the kind of person who'd be keen to follow up anything on the genealogical stuff Bernard had left him. Pam said that Harry (like me) had put it away and forgotten it. Unless, of course, there was something in it that had worried or upset him.

I went over to my desk and got out the folder of papers. There was a separate family tree for each branch of the family as well as a large, comprehensive one of the whole lot. I stared at Harry's, but it didn't really tell me anything I could make any sense of. Just him and his father and his father's elder brother and then *their* father and back to our common great-grandfather. It all seemed innocuous enough, nothing to upset anyone that I could see. Then I remembered Bernard saying to me that his research wasn't complete and if he found anything else he'd let me know. Perhaps he'd found out something else about Harry's branch of the family. Well, there might be a way of finding out.

When I rang Janet, she was quite a long time answering.

"Oh, hello, Sheila — so sorry to keep you waiting, but I was just putting a few things into a suitcase."

"You're going away?" I said, surprised.

"Just overnight. Luke rang and suggested that I might like to go up there just for the afternoon and evening. I can drive up."

"What a good idea," I said. "When are you leaving? Only there's something I wanted to ask you."

"Not till just before lunch — if I drive through the lunch hour, Luke says, there'll be less traffic. I can have something when I get there."

"Would you mind if I came round now? I won't stay long."

"Yes, of course, do come."

The Janet who opened the door to me was a quite different Janet from the person I'd left with Christine. She looked happy, for one thing, and ten years younger.

"Do come in. Shall we have a cup of coffee?"

"That would be lovely if you have time. I don't want to hold you up."

"No, that's fine — it's lovely to see you."

We chatted as she made the coffee; at least, she did most of the talking.

"It's only a one-bedroom flat they have over the restaurant," she said, "but there's a sofa bed I can have; it's quite comfortable, Luke says."

The phrase "Luke says" occurred very frequently in her conversation, and I suddenly realized what a pleasure, a relief, it must be for her to be able to speak his name openly after all these years.

"I'm so glad you're going to have this little break," I said. "I was worried about you staying alone here."

"Actually" — she leaned forward confidentially — "I'm not telling Christine I'm going back to Bristol. She probably wouldn't approve and it's only for a night, after all. Do you know I've never been into the restaurant — I've passed by it so many times, looking in, hoping to see him . . ." Her voice trailed away, but she brightened up and went on, "And I'll be able to meet Yves. Luke says he's always asking about me — isn't that nice?"

"That's lovely," I said warmly. "And you must be on your way soon, so I'll just ask the favor I wanted. Do you think I could borrow some of Bernard's research notes?"

She looked surprised, as well she might, seeing what little enthusiasm I'd shown for them before.

"It's just that Michael's interested," I said, "and there may be a few points — things that Bernard found after I saw him last . . ."

"Yes, of course," she said. "They're all in a briefcase upstairs; I'll get them for you."

She came down with the heavy briefcase

Bernard had brought with him when he visited me. "Everything's in there," she said. "They're all in order — arranged by each branch of the family. The family tree is in sections with the relevant notes attached to each one." She sounded as if she was repeating a well-learned lesson, which she probably was. "I think you'll find it all quite easy to understand."

"Did you take down all the notes?" I asked.

She shook her head. "Not all of them. Bernard had to do some of them himself when I wasn't well. But his handwriting is very clear."

"I'm sure it'll be fine. I won't keep them long."

"As long as you like," she said. "I don't want them." She stopped suddenly as if realizing what she'd said; then she continued defiantly, "Well, I don't. I was never interested in all that — and it was *Bernard's* family, after all. No, you keep them if you want to."

"Oh, no," I exclaimed, appalled at the thought of being the repository of the family archive. "I couldn't do that. Besides, Christine would probably like to keep them — after all the work her father put into them."

"I suppose so," Janet said. "But you hang on to them for as long as Michael needs them."

I thanked her and picked up the briefcase. As I turned to go I asked, "Did any other members of the family get in touch with Bernard about all this — after he called on them, I mean?"

She thought for a moment and then said, "Yes, now you mention it — Richard Prior telephoned, oh, it must have been a couple of days before Bernard — before Bernard died. He was out, so this Richard person said would I ask him to get in touch."

"And did he? Get in touch."

"No, I don't think so. Bernard said he wanted to make a few inquiries about something first. I don't know what that was all about. Oh, dear, I suppose I ought to telephone and tell them what's happened . . ."

"I'll do that, if you like," I said. "I'll get in touch with them all. You've got quite enough to worry about without going into all that."

I felt a little guilty when Janet thanked me profusely, because I thought I could use that as an excuse to see whether I could find out what, if anything, Bernard had discovered about their family secrets.

"Have a lovely time," I said as Janet came

to the door with me. "Why don't you stay for a couple of days — it would do you good."

"I might," she said. "I suppose there's nothing to stop me now, is there?"

I smiled. "Nothing at all," I said. "Tell Luke that the next time I'm in Bristol I'll look forward to visiting the restaurant and sampling his delicious food."

When I got home I laid the briefcase on the sitting room table. For a moment I felt uncomfortable seeing it there, where Bernard had put it those times he had visited, but I pulled myself together, opened it, and took out some of the folders. As I expected, each branch of the family had its own folder with a label listing its contents. I found the one for Harry Prior and opened it. Inside there was the family tree — like the one I'd already seen — and a few pages of notes made while Bernard was conducting his research. The earlier ones were in what I took to be Janet's handwriting, the later ones in Bernard's. The early ones were copies of entries in parish registers and census reports. The later notes comprised brief histories of various people in that branch of the family. These seemed much more promising.

James Prior *d.* 1936 (possibly cancer, since he was only in his fifties, though this is not stated anywhere), his wife, Martha, had died after the birth of the 2nd son (puerperal fever) in 1920. The eldest son, Robert, inherited the farm on his father's death and his younger brother, John, worked for him. At the outbreak of war Robert joined the Army and left his brother to run the farm (a reserved occupation). Before he joined up he made a will leaving everything to his brother John. No further will found. While he was stationed on Salisbury Plain he married Gloria Porter, who was working on a local farm (Marlborough registrar's records), and shortly after this he went to France with the invasion forces and was killed in Normandy (1944). His wife seems to have left the area (no mention in any census report) and there is no further information about her. Query: Any issue? John Prior *d.* 1988 leaving the farm to his only son, Harry (*b.* 1961). Further inquiries to be made.

I closed the folder and tried to work out the relevance of what I'd just read. The first thing that struck me was the question of what had happened to Robert's wife and if she'd had any children. Did Bernard make those further inquiries, and had he found out anything more that didn't appear in these notes? Was this why Harry had made that call on the day Bernard had been killed?

I got up and stretched, stiff from sitting so long, and went out into the kitchen to make myself some lunch, the animals getting up from their apparently impenetrable sleep to accompany me. I was just sitting down with my ham sandwich (I couldn't be bothered to cook anything) when Michael arrived.

"Sorry to disturb your lunch," he said, "but Thea asked me to leave these magazines for you when I was passing. She said something about a recipe."

"Oh, thank you, dear. Have you had any lunch?"

"Not really," Michael said, looking at my sandwich. "I won't really have time to get anything. I've just been to Barnstaple and I need to be back in the office in just over half an hour."

I pushed the plate towards him. "You sit down and have this and I'll make you a quick cup of coffee."

While he was drinking the coffee I said, "There's something I'd like you to look at — it won't take a moment." I went and fetched the notes from the sitting room. "These are Bernard's notes on the Priors at

Brookside Farm," I said. "What do you make of that?"

"The bit about the wife is puzzling," he said when he'd read it. "Why didn't she make some claim on the estate when Robert was killed?"

"It says that there was no new will after he got married," I said. "I don't expect there was time for him to do anything about it before he was shipped off to France. So I suppose the will he *had* made still stood."

"No," Michael said. "It would have been revoked on his marriage. That is unless he'd put in a clause along the lines of — how does it go? — 'I make this will in contemplation of matrimony to so-and-so.' Meaning, 'I still want this to stand even when I marry.' But he obviously wouldn't have put that clause in because when he made that will he didn't know he was going to marry."

"So?"

"So his widow would have inherited his estate."

"And she would be the rightful owner of the farm?"

"Yes. But the odd thing is that she never showed up." He got to his feet. "I must dash. Thanks for the lunch. See you soon."

While I was making myself another sandwich I thought about what Michael had said, the startling fact that Brookside Farm could legally belong to Robert's widow, or, since she was probably dead by now, her descendants. I wondered whether Harry *had* looked at those notes and, if so, what he'd done about it. All I knew for certain was that he'd telephoned Bernard, and there was no other reason that I could think of why he would have done that.

I suddenly remembered telling Janet that I would let people know Bernard was dead. Amazingly, the news hadn't so far appeared in the local paper — I imagine Roger had had something to do with that — so I had every reason to get in touch with Harry. I thought about telephoning, but, in the end, I felt I'd get a better idea of how things were if I went in person. I'd just drop in — on my way to somewhere or other. And I thought the morning would be the best time to find someone at home.

Next morning was bright and sunny, and this somehow gave me confidence. As I drove up to the front door, I saw that their Land Rover was parked outside, and just as I drew up Pam got out of it and came towards me.

"Hello," she said. "Have you brought Alice to see the cows?"

"No," I said. "I was just on my way to

Monksilver, so I thought I'd call in and see you. I have a bit of news."

"Come on in and have a cup of coffee. I've just been taking some cakes to sell at the W.I. Market — it earns a copper or two — but there's still one left."

She led the way into the house and settled me at the kitchen table while she put the kettle on.

"So, what's the news?"

"You remember cousin Bernard?" I said.

"Only too well."

"He's dead."

"Good heavens. When did this happen? Was it while he was down here?" She put down the knife she'd been cutting the cake with and stared at me.

"Yes, it did. As a matter of fact, I discovered him. Well, Janet — his wife, do you remember her? — and I did."

"How upsetting — it must have been awful for you. What did he die of?"

"Well, he actually died of a heart attack, but . . ." I paused. "But," I continued, "someone had tried to kill him."

"Good God!"

"I know. I couldn't believe it, but it's true."

"Who on earth would want to kill him?"

I shrugged. "Several people, apparently. He wasn't a very nice person."

"He was a dreadful bore, but still . . . Of course, we hardly knew him, so I suppose we wouldn't have known . . ." She was silent for a moment, and then she said, "But you said he died of a heart attack?"

"That's right. But the murderer didn't know he was dead — just thought he was asleep. Hit him over the head."

"But that's ghastly," Pam said slowly. "Really horrible."

"I know."

Pam moved a cup of coffee towards me and put a slice of ginger cake on a plate. "Tell me what you think," she said. "It's a new recipe." She appeared to be considering something, and then, seeming to make up her mind, she said, "Cousin Bernard gave us rather a nasty shock."

"Really?"

"You know that genealogy — family tree and all that stuff — well, I think I told you, Harry shoved it in a drawer and forgot about it. But one day, when Matt was home for the weekend, I told him about it and he said he was interested and could he have a look at it."

"Really?"

"Yes. The thing is, he discovered something really awful."

"What sort of thing?"

"As well as the family tree thing, there were some notes." She hesitated and then went on. "Harry's uncle Robert joined up in the army in the war and left Harry's father to look after the farm. Well, Uncle Robert was killed in the D-day landings in Normandy, but before he was sent to France he got married."

"How sad. What about his widow?"

"That's the thing — we never knew anything about her, nor about the marriage. Not Harry's father, not anyone. We never knew there was a widow."

"What a peculiar thing."

"It's more than peculiar; it's really worrying." Pam paused again. "You see," she said, "there may very well have been a child, and if there was, then the farm would belong to him."

"But that's dreadful," I said. "The farm is Harry's life, and Josh's too."

"Exactly."

"So what are you going to do?"

Pam gave a wry smile. "I was all for just ignoring it, letting things be. After all, no one's ever turned up claiming the farm. It was all a long time ago and — damn it all — *we've* looked after it, built it up, kept it going. It would be really unfair if anyone else came along and wanted to take it away from us, wouldn't it?"

"Absolutely. What does Harry think?"

She shook her head. "You know Harry — honest as the day is long. He said he wouldn't feel right just leaving things as they are."

"So what's he going to do?"

"Matt's got some holiday coming to him, so he's going down to Wiltshire to see what he can find out."

"That's quite a task!"

"I know. But Harry rang Bernard when all this came to light, and Bernard gave Harry the name of the farm she worked on." She sighed. "Honestly, Sheila, I'm terrified of what Matt might find out. If the farm does belong to someone else, I really don't know what's to become of us."

CHAPTER TWELVE

"I must say, I'm with Pam over this," Rosemary said when I told her what had happened. "After all, if no one's turned up for over sixty years — well, I mean!"

"Oh, I know, I feel the same, especially when they've all worked so hard to make a go of things. Not just Harry, but Josh — that's his eldest son — and Pam too. But that's Harry all over — he'd rather die than do anything he thought wasn't right."

"It's all very well being noble, but when it's your family and their livelihood at stake, I think you have to fight for it. Actually," she went on, "I'm feeling very family orientated today. That's why I called round — to tell you. I heard from Colin today. Marianne's had the baby. It's a boy — eight pounds — and they're going to call him John after Jack."

"Oh, how marvelous! Your third grandchild; aren't you lucky! You must be thrilled."

"It's lovely, but Toronto is *so* far away. It's maddening not to be able to see him; photos really aren't the same." She sighed. "It's a melancholy thought, really, that I haven't even met Marianne. When Colin told me they were getting married, I was so happy for him — after the breakup with Charlotte and all that — and I did hope they might have come over then. But Colin got this job in Toronto and they had to up sticks and move, so somehow it never happened. And now there's a grandson as well as a daughter-in-law I've never seen."

"I suppose you couldn't . . . ?"

"There's no way I could suggest it — you know what Jack's like about abroad."

"They *might* come over here," I said consolingly. "Perhaps at Christmas?"

"Oh, not with a very young baby; it wouldn't be right. No, when he's a bit older, perhaps. I mustn't grumble. After all, I've got Jilly and Roger and the children living practically on the doorstep. Lots of people have children and grandchildren living abroad. Look at poor Heather Wainwright. Her only daughter went to Ethiopia, for heavens' sake, with Médecins Sans Frontières, and goodness knows when she'll see *her* again, not to mention worrying about the danger all the time. No, I'm sure they'll come over when they can. But I do want to buy some things for the baby, so I wondered if you'd feel like coming to Taunton with me next week. We could make a day of it. I think we could both do with a treat."

We had a nice day's shopping, and as well as things for the baby, Rosemary bought several garments for Delia and her brother, Alex ("So they don't feel left out"), and I found an enchanting little dress for Alice. It's a sign of getting older, I suppose, when buying clothes for oneself is a chore but buying things for one's grandchildren is pure pleasure.

We stopped off at a pub for lunch on the way home.

"Better than Taunton," Rosemary said. "Plenty of parking space and, anyway, this place had a good write-up in *Somerset Life.*"

The pub was a bit self-consciously rural, with a real log fire in the wide hearth, a plethora of agricultural implements hung on the walls, and many sepia photographs of happy farm workers leading cart horses and wagonloads of hay. Apparently the publicity had had some effect, because it was very full and we had to wait a while for our food.

"Well, it was worth waiting for," Rosemary said, looking with satisfaction at her excellent sea bass, "and all freshly cooked, not just heated up in a microwave. How's your calf's liver?"

"Gorgeous," I said. "They've done it with sage — quite delicious."

We'd been early, so other people were still arriving when we left. I was just getting into the car when a voice behind me said, "Sheila? Sheila Malory?"

I turned and saw that it was Rebecca Prior, Richard's wife.

"I've been meaning to ring you," she said, "about this man Bernard Prior — some sort of cousin of Richard. He's being a perfect nuisance. Do you know anything about him?"

"Well, actually," I replied, "I was going to ring you. He's dead."

"Oh." She looked disconcerted. "Well, of course I'm sorry and all that . . ."

"It's a complicated story," I said. "Look, we can't go into it now — could I possibly come and see you and explain?"

"Well, yes, if you like. Would Friday do? Come to coffee, about eleven. I must dash now — I'm meeting someone for lunch and I'm late already."

She gave me a wave and a quick smile and

was gone.

I got into the car, where Rosemary was waiting patiently at the wheel.

"That was a bit of luck," I said as Rosemary looked at me inquiringly. "That was Rebecca, Richard Prior's wife. I wanted to go and see them about Bernard, and now I've arranged to go and have coffee on Friday."

Rosemary laughed. "More suspects? Poor souls; little do they know when they innocently dish out coffee invitations to you that you're doing your Miss Marple act."

"Well," I said defensively, "it seemed too good an opportunity to be missed. Anyway, she said she wanted to ask me about Bernard."

When I got home, I took out the documents for Richard from Bernard's briefcase. As before, I couldn't find anything interesting in the family tree. Richard was an only child, but his father had had a sister and two brothers, one of whom, Walter, appeared to have gone to live in America, since beside his name it said "*d.* Oregon?" The other brother, Norman, was also dead, as was Richard's father, George, but the sister, Edna, seemed to be still alive, though since she was born in 1920, she was now quite elderly. She had married a Paul Chapman ("*d.* 1987") and had a daughter, Emma. Norman ("*m.* Margaret Vesey 1970; *d.* 1994") had a son, Vernon, and he was still alive. Richard and Rebecca had one son, Charles. There seemed to be nothing particularly remarkable about all that, so I turned to the notes. But these weren't much help either. There were dates and places of birth for everyone, and dates of death of Norman and George. For Walter it merely said, "check Family Records Center Web site, also US sites to find date of death, marriage, issue, etc." All quite straightforward, but, as far as I could see, no dreadful secret that would lead to murder.

I put the papers away and went upstairs. Foss, who had been asleep on my bed since before I went out, lifted his head as I went into the bedroom.

"Are you *still* asleep?" I asked him. "Wouldn't you like to go out in the fresh air with Tris instead of frowsting in here all day?"

He gave me one of his blank stares, then putting his head on his paws and wrapping his tail around his nose once more, he went back to sleep. Rebuffed, I changed my shoes, put my coat away, and went back downstairs.

As I got down the calendar in the kitchen to make a note of my visit to Rebecca on Friday, I saw with horror that it was tomorrow I was supposed to be going to tea with Rosemary's mother, Mrs. Dudley. I had pushed it to the back of my mind — since visiting Mrs. Dudley was something not dwelt upon with anything other than apprehension — and now the time had caught up with me.

Armed with a stephanotis in a pot, I arrived on the doorstep exactly at four o'clock. This meant that I had been sitting in my car, parked round the corner, for ten minutes, since being too early was equally bad as being too late. Her housekeeper, Elsie, ushered me into the sitting room and was told sharply to bring in the tea in "a quarter of an hour exactly." Mrs. Dudley was sitting by the fire — a coal fire, naturally, since this was what she had always been used to, but in addition to, not instead of, central heating. The room was, therefore, extremely warm, and I was glad I'd remembered to put on a thin summer dress, although we were well into autumn. I advanced cautiously into the room. One never quite knew what sort of mood Mrs. Dudley would be in, and it was always advisable to test the water, as it were, before embarking on any conversation. I held out the stephanotis in a sort of propitiatory gesture and was pleased to see a smile lighten her face.

"Ah, stephanotis," she said softly. "I had some in my wedding bouquet. Thank you, Sheila; that was most thoughtful of you. Put it down somewhere where I can see it. No, *not* on that table," she added sharply. "Over there by the window. Now come and sit down and tell me all your news. I've been confined to the house in this terrible wet weather we've been having, and I haven't had a visitor for days."

This, I knew for a fact, was not strictly true, since Rosemary visited her almost every day and always spoke to her on the telephone, but I also knew that Rosemary didn't count as a proper visitor, being merely a daughter. I sat down and produced such scraps of gossip as I'd prepared in readiness for the occasion. Mrs. Dudley listened, absently for her, and then, when there was a pause, said, "And what's all this about that tiresome cousin of yours? Dead, is he?"

I realized that I should never have expected her to be ignorant of such a sensational piece of news, though I couldn't imagine how she'd heard of Bernard's death, and I knew there was no way I could ask. So I took a deep breath and gave her a full account of what had happened. She listened in silence, except that when I told her about the murder attempt after Bernard was dead she gave an involuntary exclamation.

"Well," she said when I'd finished, "I suppose I should never be surprised at what happens in this day and age, but this is beyond everything! It would appear that one isn't safe from this terrible sort of thing even when one is dead!" I gave a murmur of agreement, and she went on. "I didn't care for the man — I met him several times with his cousin, no his *second* cousin, who I knew quite well at one time. She used to be a friend of mine before she moved out of the district." Anyone who moved out of the district was automatically removed from Mrs. Dudley's list of "friends," that is, people who belonged to the Dudley mafia and were no longer useful as sources of information when they moved away.

"His second cousin?" I asked.

"Yes, Edna Chapman. A silly woman, but well meaning, I suppose. I believe she's in a home now — Alzheimer's, I expect — I'm not surprised."

"She had two brothers, didn't she?"

Mrs. Dudley settled more comfortably in her chair as she embarked on her favorite topic. "Yes, there was George — he was the eldest — then Norman; both dead now. And then there was Walter. He was much younger than the others, a very difficult person, quite wild, I believe, though," she said regretfully, "I never knew the precise details. Not that it mattered in the end, because he went to America and nobody ever heard of him again. I expect," she added confidently, "he drank himself to death."

"And what about their children?" I prompted.

"Money mad," Mrs. Dudley said. "Richard, George's boy, is some sort of surveyor — whatever that is — but he's been buying up property for years. Vernon appears to be a thoroughly unpleasant person; so I've been told, though I have never met him myself. He has a chain of garages, I believe, somewhere in Surrey. Edna's daughter, Emma, lives in London. She works on one of those women's magazines. Such a rackety life they all seem to lead, living with some man she isn't married to — Edna was very worried about her. She was afraid he was just after her money, of course."

"Money?" I asked. "Emma had a lot of

money?"

"Oh, yes, they all did."

"Really?"

"George and Norman made an absolute fortune; Edna too. There was this piece of land they all inherited jointly from their father. Quite a large area just outside Taunton. The fact is" — she leaned towards me — "their father, old William Prior, was a coal merchant." She paused to see what effect this pronouncement had on me.

"I never knew that."

"Oh, yes. There was quite a scandal about the business he'd been running; he was some sort of financial dealer, I believe. Anyway, he lost everything, absolutely everything. The next thing anyone heard, he'd got a horse and cart and was going around selling *coal.* Well, as you can imagine, the rest of the family simply washed their hands of him, and you can hardly blame them. Still," she admitted, "he was very hardworking, and in the end, he built up a very thriving business. He bought these fields for the — what do you call it? — the depot, and then adjoining ones for the horses and so on. He did very well, and he was considered to be quite a prosperous businessman when he died."

"So that's how George and the others got

their money?"

Mrs. Dudley smiled. "Oh, dear, no. It was selling the fields that did that. They sold them to a property developer who built a whole housing estate on them — you must know where I mean, the other side of Bishops Hull."

"Yes — do you mean that one? But it's vast!"

"Exactly." Mrs Dudley nodded. "*That's* where the money came from. George, Norman and Edna were very well off indeed, and so are their children."

"Well," I said again, "I never knew that."

"You certainly would never have heard from *them* — about their grandfather, I mean. They would hate to think of people knowing about him. Terrible snobs, all of them. I really can't be doing with that sort of attitude." I tried to prevent my jaw dropping at that statement, since Mrs. Dudley is, and always has been, the most snobbish person I know. "I always," Mrs. Dudley went on, "take people as I find them."

"My father never mentioned it," I said, "though I suppose he must have known. I seem to remember that he and Richard's father used to go fishing together occasionally."

"Your dear father," Mrs. Dudley said,

"was a wonderful man and an excellent clergyman — his sermons always made one *think* about things in a spiritual way, not like the dreadful socialist nonsense the present clergy give us — but he was quite other-worldly about so many things, and especially about money. I don't suppose he ever thought about where Richard and his family got theirs."

"No," I said, "I don't suppose he did. So Richard and the others used this money to build up their own business empires, I suppose."

"Money always comes to money," Mrs Dudley said. "That's what my father used to say. Edna too. Now, she married Paul Chapman — he had private means (his father owned a lot of property in the center of Bristol), and he had this large estate just outside Dulverton. I believe it sold for some extraordinary figure when they moved to Bath — he had some sort of rheumatic condition and needed permanent treatment there. No," she concluded, "there's a lot of money in that family."

"So it seems."

"Mind you, I've always said — money doesn't buy happiness." She picked up the small silver bell from the small table beside her and rang it. "I think we might have tea now."

Elsie brought in the tea and, as usual, I ate far too much, tempted on this occasion by Elsie's egg and cress sandwiches (tiny ones, so that one ate an enormous number without really noticing how many) and her heavenly apple cake. Mrs. Dudley "managed" two scones (with cream and jam), an éclair and a large slice of cake.

As I was surreptitiously loosening the belt of my dress, Mrs. Dudley said, "Of course, it was lucky for George and the others that Walter had vanished from the scene so completely. There would have been considerably less for the rest of them if they'd had to share the fortune with him. But there, Walter was always a ne'er-do-well, so he would probably have simply squandered his share, so it was probably a mercy that he never had it. "

We talked of other things after that, or rather Mrs. Dudley did, which was how she liked conversation to be, and when I rose to go she was in a mellow mood.

"It was so kind of you to spare the time to call on an old friend," she said, inclining her cheek to be kissed. "You know I am always happy to see you." She looked at me critically. "Sheila, are you quite well? You are looking very flushed."

Outside I got into the car and drove down to the seafront. As I stood looking at the sea, breathing in the blessed fresh air and relaxing from the strain of the afternoon, I considered what Mrs. Dudley had told me. The whole situation of that branch of the family was much more complicated than I'd realized. All that money. Surely that might very well be a motive for murder. Roger always said it was the first thing he thought of in a murder case. The sale of the land was obviously the key, and what that generation had done seems to have had repercussions down to the present day. In fact, it was more important to Richard and his cousins than to their parents, because that inheritance had been the foundation of their present fortunes. They would be most anxious that nothing call the inheritance into question.

I stared out across the channel to where the coastline of Wales was illuminated by sunshine lacking here. The sea was still and gray, with hardly any movement of the waters. A solitary crow pushed its way onto the rail where several seagulls were perched, and they turned on the intruder with hoarse cries and angry, open beaks. That, I thought, would be how Richard and the others would see off any other claimant to what they considered theirs. Walter and his descendants, for instance. If Bernard might have somehow roused that particular sleeping dog, then he would have been very dangerous to them indeed.

CHAPTER THIRTEEN

Richard and Rebecca now lived in what had been an old rectory in the Quantocks. They'd bought it fairly recently so I'd never visited them there before, and it took me quite a while to find it. Previously they'd lived in one of the large Georgian houses on the outskirts of Taunton. Not that I'd visited them there very often since Peter had died, and Rebecca had apparently felt that her dinner parties should consist only of couples. Not that I minded — I always found the formality of those occasions (people chosen, it seemed to me, for their usefulness rather than their entertainment value) rather wearing.

The house still preserved its identity — THE OLD RECTORY, it proclaimed — on the nameplate attached to one of the imposing stone pillars that guarded the drive. The pleasant cream stucco of the house was set off by formal flower beds and a lawn shaded by an immense ancient cedar, the whole thing so perfect as to seem almost unreal. The large iron bell set off sonorous echoes in the house when I pulled it, and I half expected some sort of butler or majordomo to open the door. But it was only Rebecca, looking elegant in shades of beige, doubtless some designer label I'd never heard of. I wished momentarily that I'd worn something more worthy than the tweed jacket and skirt and polo-necked jumper I'd considered adequate for morning coffee with a relative.

"I'm sorry I'm a bit late," I said apologetically, "but I must have taken the wrong turning at Stogumber — I'm hopeless with maps!"

"We are a little remote here," Rebecca said, "but we do like the peace and quiet. Do come in. I thought we'd have coffee in the library."

She led the way through the hall with its enormous chandelier, past the elegantly curving staircase, past a large, handsome room, apparently the drawing room, past a smaller handsome room with chairs set round a long dining table and an immense amount of silver on display, and opened a heavy mahogany door into the library. The bookcases lining the walls were of mahogany too, heavy, with carved pilasters dividing them into sections. There was a massive marble fireplace with an antique mirror above it, and on either side hung portraits of eighteenth-century gentlemen set against a landscape background, one carrying a scroll and one resting his hand on a globe. Ancestors, though whose ancestors I couldn't say, since the Prior family certainly hadn't produced them and I knew for a fact that Rebecca's family had been shoe manufacturers from Leicester and were unlikely descendants of the two assured gentlemen thus immortalized on canvas. Presumably one could buy them by the yard as I was sure Richard had bought the handsome leather-bound books that stood in complacent rows along the shelves.

Rebecca motioned me to a chair beside the fireplace. There was a real coal fire there, as there had been at Mrs. Dudley's, but here the heat given out, even though presumably supplemented by some sort of concealed heating system, was not adequate to warm the large room, such heat as there was having ascended into the recesses of the ceiling. Rebecca sat opposite me, where a tray of coffee things had been set out on a small Pembroke table.

"Black or white?" she asked.

"Oh, white, please."

Rebecca had hers black with no sugar, so I defiantly put two cubes of brown coffee sugar as well as cream into my cup.

"Richard's just had to go down to the village — arrangements about a fund-raising event for the village hall. It's so important to do what one can for the community, don't you agree? But he'll be back soon. I know he's very anxious to see you."

We made desultory conversation. At least, Rebecca made statements about various subjects and paused briefly for me to agree with her. I was forcibly reminded of Mrs. Dudley. After about ten minutes Richard came in. A small man, he nevertheless gave the impression of energy and importance by his bustling movements and forceful manner of speech.

"Well, well, Sheila. Splendid to see you — been far too long. Can't think where the time goes." He accepted a cup of coffee from Rebecca and sat down beside me. "So, what's all this about Bernard being dead? Quite a shock. He seemed perfectly well when he called on us. *That* was a surprise, I can tell you — hardly knew the man, but we were in when he rang up and couldn't very well get out of seeing him."

"He died of a heart attack," I said.

"A heart attack?" Richard looked puzzled. "He never said he had a heart condition — just about the only thing he didn't tell us. I've never known a man go *on* in such a way; thought we'd never get rid of him. Tedious." He shook his head. "Shouldn't say that, I suppose, when the man's dead."

"I don't think he knew he had a heart condition," I said. "Certainly his wife didn't know."

"I always say, everyone should have a proper checkup. Rebecca and I go every year — a good private clinic in Bristol — we call it our MOT." He laughed and I smiled politely.

"Actually, it's a bit more complicated than that," I said. "The heart attack, I mean. The fact is, someone broke in and tried to kill him — not knowing that he was already dead."

They stared at me in silence, and then Richard said slowly, "What exactly do you mean?"

I explained the circumstances of Bernard's death and they were silent again. After a moment Rebecca said, "How perfectly disgusting," and Richard said, "And *you* actually found him?"

"Yes. I'd taken Janet, his wife, back after she'd been spending an evening with me."

"How ghastly for you," Rebecca said.

Richard put down his coffee cup and leaned forward. "You say there was a break-in — it was a burglary, then?"

"From what I've gathered, the police aren't sure."

"It sounds like an open-and-shut case to me," Richard said, "unless they've got any evidence to the contrary."

"Not that I know of."

"Well, it's all very sad. A tiresome man, though, as I said, one mustn't speak ill of the dead. The thing is, I had a look at the family tree and the notes he gave us — really quite interesting — and there are a couple of things I wanted to speak to him about."

"Really?"

"Yes, a few things I'd like to pursue further. Did he do all the research himself, do you happen to know? Some of the writing was in another hand."

"Oh, that would be Janet. She took down a lot of the material for him."

"I see. And I suppose she has the notes and things now?"

For some reason, I felt I didn't want Richard to know that I had them at home.

"Yes, I imagine they belong to her now," I said.

"Is she still in Taviscombe? They were renting some sort of holiday cottage, weren't they? I think that's what Bernard said. He gave me the telephone number — I've got it somewhere."

"She went to Bristol for a couple of days," I said, "but I think she's back now. There are still arrangements to make, of course."

"Of course."

There was another silence, but this time it was the silence that a hostess employs to indicate to her guest that the visit should be drawing to a close. I got up.

"It's been so nice seeing you," I said.

They both saw me to the door, and I had the feeling that they couldn't wait to get rid of me so they could discuss what I'd told them.

"We must have lunch sometime," Rebecca said. "That pub is really excellent."

"Do come again soon," Richard said heartily. "Don't be a stranger!"

They were inside the house and had shut the door even before I'd started the car, making me quite sure that they'd found my information about Bernard in some way very disturbing.

"I must say," I said to Rosemary when I was telling her about my visit. "I'm very glad they're only *remote* relatives and I don't have to see them more than once in a blue moon."

"We all have some of those," Rosemary said with some feeling. "Jack more than most. He's got this ghastly cousin Molly. No, not a proper cousin even — she's his uncle Frank's wife's daughter from *her* first marriage. Anyway, she — Molly, that is — was married to a diplomat, and she's lived all round the world at embassies in unimaginable splendor and — well — *condescending* isn't the word! Now that he's retired, they live in 'a *tiny* flat near Harrods.'" Rosemary's voice took on a sharper edge. "Tiny! It's a vast apartment in Hans Place, crammed with antiques. All the carpets are inches thick and *white*. They have a grand party once a year that Jack makes us go to — you know what he's like about family — and I absolutely dread it. Dreadful woman! She always makes me feel like a clumsy, ill-dressed *peasant!*"

"Well," I said fairly, "I don't think Rebecca's as bad as that, but pretty annoying all the same. Anyway, I'm sure there's something sinister about the way they've reacted to Bernard poking around in the family archive. Richard seemed jolly keen to get his hands on Bernard's notes. Not, actually, that there's anything specific in them, though Richard isn't to know that."

"Long-lost heirs?" Rosemary asked. "Like in Victorian novels or Australian soaps?"

"Well, yes, as a matter of fact, there is something a bit like that. Richard's father had two brothers and a sister, and one of the brothers went to America and doesn't seem to have been heard of again. Apparently he went off in rather dubious circumstances, so your mother says."

"Mother would know," Rosemary said.

"Anyway, Richard's father, George, and the other two inherited some land from their father that they were able to sell for a fabulous sum, which is the foundation of all their fortunes. I haven't seen the will, of course, but I bet Bernard did, and if their father simply left his property equally to all his children, then Walter should have had a share of that money. The question is, did they try to find him, or not? If they conveniently forgot all about him, or genuinely believed that he was dead, then they wouldn't be too happy to have Bernard uncovering things they'd rather have forgotten."

"You think Richard might have killed him?"

"Richard or his cousins. The other uncle

is dead and the sister's in a home, but all three of *them* would have a motive."

"Where do the others live?"

"According to your mother (again), Vernon lives in Surrey and Emma is in London."

"So, really, Richard is the most likely one to have done something, being on the spot, you might say."

"That's right. Now that I come to think of it, he was a bit odd when I told him about Bernard having been dead already. *And* he was very quick to say that he thought it must have been a burglary."

"Well," Rosemary said, "if there is all that money involved, it does seem to be a pretty hefty motive."

"Exactly. Mind you," I went on, "it's possible that if Walter went off to America in disgrace, then his father might have cut him out of his will altogether."

"Actually," Rosemary said, "if there was a will, the solicitor would have known about this Walter, wouldn't he? And surely he'd be obliged to advertize for him and all that — you know, you see notices in the paper in those legal columns that nobody ever reads. Perhaps they did all that and never got a reply, so they assumed he was dead."

"And then," I broke in, "Bernard may

have found an entry for him on one of these Web sites — they're full of Americans trying to find their roots — something, anyway, that would prove that he'd been alive at the time of his father's death and may even have descendants who'd have a claim on all that money!"

"It's quite possible." Rosemary said. "The question is, what are you going to do about it?"

"What I ought to do, I suppose, is try and find out if Richard has an alibi for the night Bernard died. But I can't imagine how I'm going to do that, short of asking him straight out."

"I expect something will occur to you," Rosemary said, getting up. "I must go. I promised Mother I'd get one of those knee support things for her from Boots — I should have done it yesterday but I didn't get round to it, so my name will be mud. And she'll go on again about what we're going to do about our ruby wedding. I suppose we'll have to have some sort of a do — Mother seems to envisage something on the lines of the jubilee celebration — and it's hopeless trying to talk to Jack about it, because all he says is, 'Do whatever you think fit,' which is no help at all."

"Have you thought where?"

"Mother says it has to be the Castle in Taunton, but I really don't want everyone to have to go all that way, especially in the evening, and if they've got to drive (which is the only way of getting there) then no one will be able to have anything to drink — or at least the wives won't. Honestly, it's all getting to be too much trouble!"

"I'm sure we can find somewhere local," I said, "if we put our minds to it."

"Well, have a think, then. I *must* go. Let me know how you get on with Richard."

When Rosemary had gone, I had a go at trying to find Walter Prior on some of the genealogy Web sites, but it was obviously going to take so long to get anywhere, and I became dreadfully confused with the variety of entries and the possible entries, and the dates all seemed wrong, and, after a while, I began to get a headache (which always happens when I try to find anything on the Internet), so I gave the whole thing up.

While all this was in my mind I rang the cottage to see whether Janet was back from Bristol.

"I stayed *much* longer than I meant to," she said, "but the boys were so kind and welcoming and everything was so marvelous that the time simply flew."

It took me a moment to adjust to this new,

bubbly Janet.

"I'm so glad it was a success," I said.

"Oh, it was wonderful, and it'll be so good to be able to go and see them when I get back."

"When are you going?" I asked.

"Well" — she paused — "Christine wants the funeral in Bristol next week. She's making the arrangements — she wanted to do it and I'm sure she'll manage better than I could. I don't know the exact day yet, but I'll let you know when I do. I know it's rather a journey for you, but I do hope you'll be able to come."

"Yes, of course I will, and I'm glad you're here for a few more days, because I hope you might feel like coming to supper tomorrow — you can tell me all about Luke and the restaurant."

"That would be lovely; thank you so much."

"Oh, good. About seven thirty, then?"

When I put the phone down, I sat thinking for a while. I was glad Janet was going back to Bristol, to her new, happy life, but in a way, I felt that her going somehow made it less likely that I'd find out now who tried to kill Bernard. Which was silly, since obviously Janet had nothing to do with his death and I was sure there was nothing more she could tell me that might be of any use in what was, perhaps, a pointless investigation. Tris, who'd been sitting patiently by my side, decided it was time I attended to my duty and nudged my ankle with his cold, wet nose. So I got up and put my coat on, and we went for a brisk walk over the hill, where the wind blew away any irritating thoughts.

I'd made a stroganoff for supper and, looking at the clock, I was wondering when to start cooking the rice. But the time went on. Seven o'clock, seven thirty, seven forty-five. I went out into the kitchen and turned off the oven, then I picked up the phone and dialed Janet's number, but all I got was the answering machine, so I assumed she'd left. But where was she?

By nine o'clock I was really worried and wondering whether I could get Luke's number from directory assistance, until I remembered that I didn't know the name of the restaurant. The animals, sensing my agitation, were restless too. Foss in particular refused to settle, and prowled round the room, complaining loudly that things weren't as usual. Eventually he came and sat on my lap, but he didn't go to sleep as he always did, instead lying there with his eyes wide open. When the phone rang he leapt down, digging his claws into my knee as he did so. I was as startled as he was and snatched at the phone, saying, "Janet, where are you? Are you all right?"

The voice at the other end was not Janet's.

"Hello, Mrs. Malory, this is Sandra at Casualty. Mrs. Prior asked me to telephone you; she was afraid you'd be worried."

"What's happened?"

"I'm afraid she's been in an accident and is quite badly hurt."

"An accident?"

"Yes. A car accident."

"And badly hurt, you say? How bad?"

Sandra paused for a moment, and I wondered whether she would give me any details. But we were old acquaintances from my work with the Hospital Friends.

"Well, actually" — she lowered her voice — "she's going to be moved to Taunton; we're just waiting for the ambulance. She's got a couple of broken ribs, a lot of bad bruising and possible concussion."

"Can I come and see her?"

"Well, as I say, she's being moved to Taunton; and really she's very shaken, so no visitors at the moment. But you could phone Taunton tomorrow if you like."

"Thank you so much for letting me know, Sandra — I was getting very worried. A car accident, did you say? What happened?"

"Well, she wasn't making a lot of sense, but she said she had to swerve because this other car drove straight at her and she went into a tree. Honestly, she's lucky to be alive."

CHAPTER FOURTEEN

When I phoned the hospital in Taunton the next morning, they said Janet was "comfortable" (which never inspires confidence) but I could visit her. I found her in a side ward. Her face was badly cut and bruised and she looked pale and anxious. I put the magazines I'd brought on the bed and sat down beside her.

"What an awful thing to have happened. How *are* you?"

She managed a wan smile and said, "They keep telling me how lucky I am, but I don't really *feel* lucky. No, that's not fair — I could have had all sorts of terrible internal injuries, but, thank goodness, I don't."

"Thank goodness, indeed! But you must be in a lot of pain."

"The other good thing is that the ribs are cracked and not broken — if they had been, there was a possibility that they might have damaged the lung. And they're giving me lots of pain relief, so they're right, I have been lucky."

"So what happened?"

"Would you mind pouring me some water, please? I can't really stretch to reach it. Thanks so much." She took a sip of water and continued. "I left the cottage to visit you at about seven o'clock. It was quite dark by then and a bit misty, but I could see perfectly well. I was just approaching that sharp bend — you know the one, on the hill, towards the end of the lane — when a car came round the corner going very fast. The lane's a bit narrow, but there was plenty of room for it to pass, but it simply came straight at me. I couldn't believe it. I thought it would move over, but it didn't; it kept coming on. So I wrenched the wheel over to avoid it and drove into a tree. I must have blacked out, because the first thing I remember was an ambulance man asking me my name." She took another sip of water. "It was so frightening, Sheila, really horrible."

"It must have been. And, yes, you've been very lucky indeed."

"The police came this morning. That nice sergeant we saw before. I suppose it was because the accident happened in his area. Anyway, it made it easier when it was someone I'd seen before."

"Yes, he's a nice man. What did he say?"

"He said it was probably joyriders — why do they call them that! — and they'd be investigating. The trouble was, I couldn't give them any sort of description of the car or the driver — I mean, it was dark and all I saw were the headlights coming toward me —" She broke off in distress.

"So have you been able to get in touch with Luke or Christine," I asked, to change the subject, "or would you like me to do it for you?"

"No, it's all right, there's a phone here I could use. I called Christine. I didn't want to worry Luke, but perhaps you could ring him. Just tell him I'm all right and will be coming home soon."

"Really?"

"They want me to stay here for another day, then Christine's arranged for me to go into a nursing home in Clifton, just until I can manage on my own. I wanted to go straight home, but — well, you know what she's like and I didn't want to upset her arrangements."

"I think it's a good idea," I said, "and Luke can visit you there."

She brightened up. "Yes, so he can. Have you got something to write on? I'll give you his address and phone number. Are you sure you don't mind?"

"No, of course not."

Janet gave me the paper with Luke's number and said, "Oh, there is one other thing, if you wouldn't mind. I had a call from Bernard's relation Richard Prior, who wanted to ask me about some notes. He asked if he could come and see me yesterday evening, but I said I was going to see you, so he said would this evening be all right, and I said yes. But, of course, if I'm in here . . ." She paused and went on. "They don't really like you to use the hospital phone for nonurgent calls, so I wonder if you could ring him and explain that I won't be there?"

"Of course," I said. "No problem."

The fact that Richard wanted to know more about Bernard's notes seemed to me highly significant, and I was still wondering about this, threading my way through the parked cars and dodging the ambulances outside the hospital, when I came face to face with Roger.

"Hello," he said, "have you been visiting your cousin?"

"Cousin's widow, actually," I said. "Yes, I have. What about you?"

"I'm on my way to visit her too," Roger said. "I saw Sergeant Harris's report and I thought I'd just have a word."

"Really? So *you* think there may have been some connection between what happened to Janet and Bernard's murder."

"Attempted murder," Roger said, "since we're both being pedantic. I don't really think anything, but, since she's in Taunton and so am I, it seemed sensible to see what she had to say."

"Do you have a minute? I'd like to have a word with you myself."

"Sure. Shall we sit down on this bench, given apparently," he said, looking down at a plaque attached to it, "in memory of Samuel Pride Davis — what a peculiar place to want to put a memorial bench! I wonder if he died here and his not-so-loving relatives put it up in gratitude?"

"Not necessarily. They may have saved his life and he put it here himself. Anyway," I continued, sitting down, "it's about Janet and the accident."

"Yes?"

"It seems to me that if Bernard's murder — all right, attempted murder — wasn't the result of a burglary that went wrong, then it must have been because, in the course of all his digging into family history — and he did dig in the most tremendous detail — he may have uncovered something that somebody would rather have kept hidden."

Roger nodded. "I'm with you so far. Go on."

"He gave each branch of the family he'd been investigating the big family tree, but also their own particular part of it *and* the notes he'd made about them. Now, if whoever it was thought they'd silenced Bernard, then, after a bit, realized that Janet had also been involved in making the notes and helping Bernard with the research, then they could have realized that *she* might be equally dangerous to them."

"And so," Roger said, "she had to be silenced too?"

"It's possible," I said.

"As you say, it's a possibility, and I'll bear it in mind. This whole accident thing may only be a coincidence, of course, but still . . ."

For a moment I thought of telling him about Richard's suspicious behavior, but then I decided to wait a bit. Roger looked at me quizzically.

"Sheila, there's that look on your face — is there something you're not telling me?"

I laughed. " 'His lordship with his customary detective ability . . .' " I quoted. "Yes, there is something, but it may very well be nothing. But if it *is* something, then

I'll tell you."

"Fair enough. Incidentally, the inquest will probably be adjourned for a bit, especially since Mrs. Prior is injured, so you won't be bothered with that for a while. Anyway, Sheila, I'll leave you to carry on with your own particular form of digging and rely on you to tell me if you unearth anything you think I should know." He got up. "I'd better go and visit the invalid and see if there's anything *she* can tell me. Good hunting!"

When I got home I rang Luke, and he was very agitated and annoyed at what he called Christine's high-handed arrangements.

"Mother should have come here; we could have looked after her here perfectly well until she was able to go home."

"I think," I said tentatively, "your mother's quite happy to go into this nursing home for a bit. She didn't want you to be worried, and I know *she* would be worried if you had to look after her, knowing how busy you are. You can always go and spend time with her every day when you have a spare hour or so. And she'll have proper medical attention."

"I suppose so. How is she, though? Is it serious? Tell me again what happened."

I went over all the details again, and he became a little calmer.

"How's she getting to Bristol?" he asked. "She obviously can't drive."

"She certainly can't do that, and anyway, I'm afraid the car's a total write-off. I imagine Christine has made arrangements for that too. Though, come to think of it, I could drive her down. It's not that far and I can do it there and back easily in a day."

"Would you? That would be marvelous. Look, if you do, please come to the restaurant — lunch on the house. It's the least I can do after all you've done."

"That would be lovely. I'll be in touch."

I rang the hospital and told the sister on the ward what I proposed to do. She said I could pick Janet up about ten thirty, after the consultant had seen her. She also said she would phone Christine and tell her about the change of plan, which was a relief to me, because I wasn't keen to be the one to inform her that I'd upset the arrangements.

Since I was going to be out for the whole day, I rang Thea and told her what had happened and asked whether she'd call in and check on the animals for me and take Tris for a short walk.

"Goodness, what a dreadful thing," Thea said. "Poor woman, after all she's been through already. Is she going to be all right?"

"They seem to think so. She was very lucky. Anyway, I think she'll be safer back in Bristol."

"Do you think someone did it deliberately, then?"

"I don't know, but it does seem like a strange coincidence. If someone *did* want to cover up some dark deed in the past — well, she must have known as much about it all as Bernard."

"Where are all these dangerous papers now?"

"As a matter of fact, I've got them. I borrowed them from Janet a little while ago."

"You be careful," Thea said. "Give them back to her straightaway!"

"No one knows I've got them. At least I don't think they do. But I don't want to give them back quite yet."

"Oh, don't say you're still *investigating.* The wretched man died of a heart attack."

"But, nevertheless, someone tried to kill him," I said. "It's still attempted murder."

"Well, for goodness' sake, be careful," Thea repeated. "And yes, of course I'll look in and see to things."

When I rang Richard to tell him about Janet, all I got was the answering machine, which was annoying, because I wanted to try to judge from his voice what he made of my report of the accident and the news that she was alive and well.

It was a good drive down to Bristol, not too many lorries or roadworks, and I found the nursing home quite easily. It was up on the Downs and seemed very pleasant. Full marks to Christine. When I'd seen Janet settled in and promised to give reassuring messages to Luke, it was nearly twelve thirty, so I went in search of his restaurant. It was in a small parade of shops in a good residential area, but I could see why Luke longed for a more prestigious location. I couldn't see in properly from the outside since the windows were hung with dark red curtains, hung French bistro style, from large rings. The name *Yves* was written in flowing handwriting on the glass (they would have been foolish not to make the most of the French connection), and the general appearance was definitely appealing.

Inside there were plain white walls hung with just a few black-and-white etchings, starched white tablecloths and napkins, small vases of well-chosen flowers, and dark wood high-backed chairs. The atmosphere was calm and peaceful — I was glad to see that there was no nonsense about being able to see into the kitchen (one doesn't expect to see backstage at a theater), and the general effect was one of understated elegance. Although it was quite early, several tables were already occupied. A tall, dark young man came towards me.

"Madame?"

I explained who I was, and he said, "Ah, Madame Malory, you are very welcome." He settled me at one of the best tables and unfolded my napkin with a flourish. "Luke will be with you very soon, but you will have a glass of wine while you wait. We have a charming Pouilly-Fuissé you will like, I think."

"That will be lovely," I said, slightly overwhelmed by all this attention. "But please don't bother Luke; I'm sure he must be very busy."

He smiled and hurried away, returning shortly with an open bottle and a wine cooler. He poured a glass of wine and put the bottle in the cooler beside me. The wine was, of course, absolutely delicious. As I was enjoying it, the middle-aged man at the next table leaned over and said, "Splendid place, this. We come here every Friday evening, my wife and I, and I come for lunch twice a week when I can. Wonderful food, wonderful service!"

"Yes," I said, a little taken aback at his conversation, but pleased to learn that Luke obviously had a faithful clientele. "It is delightful."

"Lovely atmosphere. The personal touch makes all the difference. Luke always comes out at the end of the evening and talks to his customers, asks what they think of the various dishes. And that chap Yves, got the French flair, if you know what I mean. Everything done properly; can't fault them on anything. This your first time here?"

"Yes, I don't live in Bristol. Actually, I'm a friend of Luke's mother. She was very anxious I should come."

"Couldn't do better!" He broke off as Luke came out of the kitchen and approached my table.

"Mrs. Malory. I'm so glad you could make it." He sat down and said quietly, "How is she?"

"Very well, considering. She's really got off lightly, and she stood up to the journey very well and seems most comfortable in the nursing home — Normanhurst, it's called, up on the Downs. I don't really know how long she'll be in there. But I imagine you'll be going to see her."

"I can go this afternoon, as soon as the lunch sitting's finished," he said. "But I'm neglecting you. What will you have to eat? There is a game terrine and to follow I can recommend the sole Veronique. It's sole today and sea bass — I only decide which fish to have when I know what's fresh in. Or there is a classic coq au vin — Yves's grandmother's recipe. But I can bring you a menu and you can see for yourself."

"No, really. It all sounds delicious. Just the sole for me, please. Are all your dishes French?"

"Yes. That is what I first learned to cook, and that is our speciality. People seem to like it."

"Your mother says you had a marvelous write-up in one of the Sunday papers."

"Yes, it did help a lot. It did make me realize what we could do in a better position. I mean, we have our faithful regulars." He turned and smiled at the man at the next table, who smiled and raised his glass in return. "But we can't do the volume here in this tiny place." He got up. "I'm sorry, I mustn't go on, keeping you waiting for your food like this."

He went off into the kitchen and Yves brought me some gorgeous home-made bread and a dish of pale Normandy butter. "It will be a little while, you understand." he said. "The fish, it must be cooked to eat immediately." I reluctantly refused another glass of wine, knowing that I had to drive back, but sat peacefully enjoying the atmosphere. The restaurant was filling up now, and there was a cheerful buzz of conversation. The man at the next table, having finished his lunch, got up to go and as he passed me he asked, "What are you having?"

I told him I was having the sole and he nodded approvingly. "Excellent. I always have fish here when it's on the menu. Mind you, in the evenings they do a marvelous casserole of pigeon and that special French thing — cassoulet, it's called. You must come and try that." He nodded and went out and I reflected that with word-of-mouth recommendations like that, Luke was well on the way to success.

The sole was perfect, as was the *poire* Hélène that followed it. When I had finished and Luke had refused to allow me to pay the bill, he said, "Would you like to look round?" I agreed eagerly and followed him into the kitchen, which was simultaneously very up-to-date and somehow traditional. I admired the gleaming stainless steel apparatus but noticed with pleasure the old, well-used, battered omelette pans and roasting dishes. Like all small restaurant kitchens,

I imagine, it seemed cramped and dark with only one window at the back. Looking out of this I saw a paved yard and a shed ("Where we house the big freezer," Luke said) and, partly covered by a tarpaulin, the motorbike he'd traveled down to Taviscombe on. But there were also pots of herbs and a couple of large planters filled with late-blooming lavender. I found this attempt to soften a bleak area somehow touching.

Luke led the way out of the kitchen, along a passage to some stairs. Upstairs there was a surprisingly spacious sitting room, and I admired the high, molded ceilings and big sash windows.

"It's a Victorian building," Luke said, "so we do have the advantage of well-proportioned rooms. It helps with the restaurant space too, of course."

The walls were white with watercolors of French scenes ("Yves is the artist here," Luke said fondly), and the furniture was modern and well chosen.

"It's very comfortable," Luke said, indicating the sofa bed, "but," he continued ruefully, "I do see that it wouldn't be suitable for an invalid. No, I have to admit that Christine was right and that Mother will be better off in the nursing home. Actually," he said, and paused as if a thought had suddenly struck him. "Actually," he repeated slowly, "I suppose that when she goes home, I'll be able to visit her — there."

"I suppose you will," I said.

"You don't know how strange it is for me to be able to say that. Home," he repeated. "I can see her at home."

CHAPTER FIFTEEN

As I drove home I considered with pleasure Janet and Luke's new life together. It seemed like a real happy ending. I pulled myself up short. A happy ending that was the result of Bernard's death. If only, I thought, Bernard had simply died of a heart attack and there'd been no (unnecessary, as it turned out) attempt on his life, how much simpler and easier it would all have been. Well, at least Janet and Luke, who'd benefit most from his death, were above suspicion. Janet had been with me, and Luke had been in his restaurant. He'd called Christine from there and, anyway, he'd been in the kitchen all evening, cooking that delicious food, and then been in the restaurant talking to the customers. I was glad about that. Anyway, if Janet's car crash *was* deliberate and an attempt to get rid of her, then that cleared them both conclusively.

Which seemed to leave Harry and Richard. Both of them had a strong motive to want Bernard silenced. I wasn't sure, though, how I'd find out whether they had alibis. Presumably Roger could do that, but I wasn't sure just how much I wanted to tell him about the results of my digging so far. I thought I might find some excuse for ringing Pam, but it would be more difficult to manufacture a reason for getting in touch with Rebecca.

The need to pass a seemingly endless convoy of lorries meant I had to concentrate on my driving, and I postponed any further thoughts until I was safely home. Actually, I'd only just got back — fed the animals (furious at my absence) and let them out into the garden — when the phone rang. It was Pam.

"Sheila," she said, "can you come over sometime? Tomorrow, if you can. There's something I want to tell you."

"Of course. When?"

"About ten thirtyish?"

"Fine."

We sat in the kitchen as usual, and Pam poured the coffee and pushed a plate towards me.

"Shortbread," she said. "I used a higher proportion of corn flour and I think it's an improvement. What do you think?"

I bit into the shortbread, which, like all Pam's baking, was superb. "Wonderful," I said. "Can I beg the recipe?"

"Sure, I'll write it out for you." She drank a little of her coffee and said, "Do you remember what I told you about the farm and Uncle Robert, and how Matt was going to try and find out about it?"

I nodded. "And did he? Find out anything?"

"Yes, he did. He was very lucky. I think I told you about this girl — her name was Gloria Porter, by the way — and we had the name of the farm where she was billeted. Anyway, Matt went to the farm, but it'd changed hands and no one there knew anything at all. He was a bit fed up about this, but he went into the post office in the nearest village — well, it was a sort of village shop and post office, where everyone knows everyone's business — and asked there, and they told him about an elderly woman in the village who might remember something. And it was amazing; she'd been a land girl on the same farm and knew this Gloria well."

"What a marvelous piece of luck."

"Wasn't it! Apparently she'd married one of the local lads and stayed down there after the war."

"So did she know what had happened to Gloria?"

"It's a very sad story, really," Pam said. "It was one of those wartime weddings when they only had a few days together before he went back to his unit. Matt said he thought that leave was cut short because of the invasion preparations and everyone had to be back in camp for security reasons."

"Of course."

"Well," Pam continued, "because it was all such a rush, her parents couldn't come down for the wedding so she went up to London — Camberwell, I think it was — to tell them all about it. But while she was there the house was destroyed by a flying bomb and they were all killed."

"How awful!"

"Robert never heard about it because the invasion had started, and so, of course, *she* never knew that he'd been killed in action."

"Oh, that's terrible," I said, "really sad."

"I know," Pam replied, "and I felt really mean about being relieved when Matt told us."

"Relieved? Oh, yes, of course — sorry, I was just thinking of it as a story. I'd sort of forgotten what it must mean to you all."

"It means that the farm really is ours; no one else has a claim to it."

"I'm so pleased for you," I said. "Not everyone would have made those inquiries. They'd just have ignored the whole thing."

Pam smiled. "That's not Harry's way. Too honest for his own good, I sometimes think."

"Still," I said, "this time honesty really did pay off. And well done, Matt, for investigating!"

"Actually," Pam said, "it's really a good thing that he did. I mean, once we knew about Uncle Robert and the marriage, if we hadn't tried to find out, then we'd always be wondering if someone was going to turn up out of the blue."

Another happy ending, I said to myself as I drove home, but again, a happy ending because of someone's death — well, two people's deaths in this case. Still I was so glad that things had turned out well for Pam and Harry.

"Mind you," I said to Rosemary when I told her the end of the story, "at the time, when Bernard was still alive, they must have felt threatened, so they did *have* a motive for wanting him out of the way."

"That's true," Rosemary agreed. "But, no, after the way Harry's behaved over all this, I simply can't believe he could have tried to kill Bernard."

"Absolutely not," I said, "and, anyway, we both know Harry; he's just not capable of doing something like that. It was silly of me to imagine that he could. So," I continued, "that leaves Richard. I'd much rather it was him!"

"Oh," Rosemary exclaimed, "I forgot to tell you. He's got an alibi."

"Who? *Richard?* How do you know?" I demanded.

"Well," Rosemary said, "I suddenly remembered that on the night your cousin Bernard died, Jack had a Rotarians meeting. You know, Richard's on the committee too, so I asked Jack if he was there, and he was. The thing started at seven thirty (such a tiresome time, so inconvenient for eating!) and didn't finish until nearly nine. Well, you know what they're like when they start arguing about something; no one will ever give way. And Richard was there all the time."

"And I suppose," I said, "*that* means he wasn't the person who caused Janet's car accident either. Oh, bother! He was quite the most promising suspect. I don't suppose Rebecca . . . no, not possible. Not hitting someone over the head, too down-to-earth. So that's that, then."

"That's everybody?"

I nodded. "Yes — except for Cousin Sibyl."

"Sibyl?"

"Now Sister Veronica."

"You mean the one that joined that Anglican order."

"That's right. They run a retirement home just outside Lynton."

"Oh, I know; one of Mother's friends — Mrs. Savage, you remember her — went in there. Mother went to visit her."

"Really?"

"Only once to see what it was like. She said it was very well run and comfortable and all that."

"But?"

"But apparently there's a chapel there and everyone's expected to go to services twice a week."

"That seems fair to me," I said. "I mean, you presumably have *some* idea of what you're letting yourself in for if you go into a home run by nuns. It's like people who put their children into church schools because of the good academic standards and then complain that they're being taught religion!"

"I don't think Mother has ever grasped the idea of an Anglican order," Rosemary said. "I believe she thinks you can't be a nun unless you're an RC. And I gather she was put out to find the nuns weren't wearing long black robes and those great white headdresses. They looked more like *nurses,* she said, and what's the point of that?"

I laughed. "Oh, well, I suppose I might go and see Sibyl. Not that I imagine for a moment *she* would have had anything to do with Bernard's death. Still, it would be interesting to see the place. I don't really know what the form is; obviously I can't just drop in. I'd better write and find out when visiting hours are, or whatever."

So I wrote a brief note to Sybil and got a reply back by return saying that she'd love to see me and would two thirty the following Tuesday be all right. I got out Bernard's material once again and looked at what he had written for Sybil. It was just the family tree, our common grandparents and then her father ("Francis Prior *m.* Elinor Partridge"), and then the entries for Sybil and her younger sister, Alma ("*m.* Howard Osborne"), and her son, Robin. There were no notes, so either he hadn't had time to investigate that particular branch, or there was nothing worth reporting. But that didn't seem like Bernard, who seemed determined to wring the last little drop of information from every single member of the family.

As always, when I'd spent any time poring over Bernard's findings, I felt the beginnings of a headache coming on, so, although it wasn't a very nice day, dull and gray with an insidious, chilly wind, I thought a little fresh air might help. Tris, who'd already encountered the weather when he went out into the garden, remained in his basket when I dangled his lead temptingly before him, but I thought that he needed the exercise so I turfed him out, saying he could stay in the car if it was too bad. Foss, comfortably ensconced on the work-top beside the radiator, gave him a look in which pity and contempt were equally mingled.

Actually, it wasn't too bad down by the sea, and Tris soon forgot his reluctance, running about on the beach investigating the pools left by the receding tide, getting (probably purposely) wet and muddy. Apart from the usual flock of gulls, Tris and I had the beach to ourselves, which is always nice, and I enjoyed watching the waves creaming onto the shore, but after a while, the wind got stronger and more unpleasant. Tris began to whimper, and as a sudden squall of rain caught me, I felt a bit like whimpering myself, so we made our way back to the promenade as quickly as we could and sat down in one of the shelters to recover our breath. I was just remonstrating with Tris, who was shaking himself vigorously all over my ankles, when someone else came into the shelter.

"Hello, Sheila. I might have known nobody else would be mad enough to come out on a day like this." It was Roger.

"Except you," I said. "Why aren't you out detecting things or filling in forms or whatever you do nowadays?"

He laughed. "Between meetings," he said. Roger often came down to the seafront whenever he had an hour to spare; he said it was a good place to think. It was another thing we had in common. "I didn't expect this, though," he said, looking at the heavy rain bouncing off the pebbles on the beach.

"I can give you a lift back, if you like," I said. "Oh, by the way, did you get anything useful from Janet about her car crash?"

He shook his head. "Not really. It was dark and she obviously panicked. She said she really didn't get a proper look at the driver, which is a nuisance because we've got him, and a witness statement would be helpful."

"You've got him?" I echoed.

"Well, *them,* really, I suppose. Sergeant Morris was right, it was joyriders. A couple of kids he's had trouble with before. He found the car, and their prints were all over it, *and* the paint marks matched the paint on Mrs. Prior's car — it was an open-and-shut case, really, but it would have helped if she'd got a look at them. Still, there's no doubt it was them. It isn't the first time they've driven someone off the road like that, so I *hope* they'll get put away, but of course, they're both underage so . . ."

"So it was an accident," I said slowly.

Roger looked at me quizzically. "I'm sorry to spoil your nice complicated theory, but yes, it was an accident, and there was no attempt to silence Janet Prior for whatever reason you may have thought."

"I suppose not," I said slowly.

"Have you run out of ideas?" Roger asked.

I nodded. "More or less," I said. "Perhaps it *was* just a burglary that went wrong after all."

"One should never reject the obvious."

"Though you did say," I went on, "that it looked too good to be true."

"Which just goes to show," Roger said, "that even I can't be right every time. So, now what? Are you giving up on it? I'm sure you have other things to do with your time."

I sighed. "It's given up on me, really," I said. "I seem to have come to the deadest of dead ends."

Tris, who'd been lying quietly at my feet, suddenly got up and almost pulled the lead out of my hand as he made a dive for a seagull that had ventured almost inside the shelter. There was a great flapping of wings on the part of the seagull and barking from Tris.

"I suppose I really ought to be getting back," Roger said. "It's still tipping down, so I'd be glad of that lift."

So I decided that I'd put the whole business of Bernard's death out of my mind, and for several days I had the feeling that there was an uncomfortable space in my life, but then other things drifted in to fill it. Anthea, for instance.

"Sheila, you haven't forgotten the committee meeting on Monday to discuss the Christmas Fayre, have you? We're practically into November now, and you know how long it takes to get anyone to commit themselves to do anything." She took a breath and went on. "Now, it's very important that we make it quite clear at the outset that Agnes Howell is *not* to be allowed to organize the collection of the mince pies. You will remember last year what a dreadful muddle she made of it. She completely underestimated the number of people who needed to supply them, and it was only because I happened to have an extra batch in my freezer that we had enough for the teas. And those frightful ones that Moira made with that stone-ground wholemeal flour — hard as bullets; no one touched them! No, I'd like *you* to organize them this year, Sheila, and make sure that Doris Makepeace brings hers on time this year. Up to the last minute we weren't sure if she was going to . . ."

By the time I'd extricated myself from all the burdens that Anthea was planning to put on me, my head was full of anything but Bernard's affairs. Then there was Rosemary.

"What do you think about that country house hotel outside Simonsbath? Cynthia said that they did Stephanie's wedding very well, but that was in the summer, of course, and most of it was outdoors. Perhaps it isn't the right place for December. Oh, dear, I do wish we'd been married in the summer; it would be so much more convenient! Of course, Mother's still going on about having it at the Castle, but I really don't . . . though, come to think of it, Simonsbath's quite a way to travel for a lot of people, and if the weather's bad some of those roads are practically impassable. Honestly, I wish to goodness people didn't make such a fuss about having been married for forty years — and all to do again, if we make it to fifty!"

Alice needed my attention too.

"Now, you be the shopkeeper and I'm the lady coming in with her little girl. We want some cakes, please (these sweeties are the cakes), and some rice (it's real rice; Mummy gave it to me), and you weigh it out on the scales. Half a pound of rice. Gran, what's tuppeny rice? Can you sing me the song? And I want two apples — we have to pretend the apples — my little girl likes apples, but she likes strawberries better. Do you like strawberries, Gran? Do you like strawberries better than apples? . . ."

Not to mention the animals. Foss, who is normally an enthusiastic eater, cleaning up his own dish and licking round Tris's empty bowl in case some fragment has been overlooked, suddenly went off his food. For two days, although he seemed perfectly healthy (cold, wet nose, full of energy), he didn't eat a thing. At first I thought he'd been catching mice and birds, but there were no pathetic little piles of feathers and no solitary mouse's gall bladder on the doormat (his usual offering). I couldn't understand it and began to be really worried. But then, suddenly, he was his usual voracious self and ate everything I offered and asked for more. Another feline mystery. Such are the maddening ways of cats, using up your time and energy, never coming when called, then strolling in hours later, totally unconcerned — "Were you calling me?" — when you've been out combing the highways and byways, peering down rabbit holes in anxiety and despair.

No, I decided, my life was full enough. After I'd been to see Sybil, I'd wipe the whole Bernard mystery completely from my mind. The trivial round, the common task, as Dr. Keble tells us, should be *quite* enough for me.

CHAPTER SIXTEEN

Tuesday was another cold day, dull and misty, with a fine drizzle falling, and I began to wonder why on earth I was going out in this miserable weather to see Sybil, someone I really didn't actually *need* to see, when I could be cozily at home occupying myself in a more rational way. The animals too showed no signs of wanting to venture out. After breakfast Tris had retired to his basket with an ancient bone for company. Foss had gone to ground under the duvet on my bed and was visible only as a motionless hump. Feeling a strong desire to join him, I nevertheless put on my warm winter coat and gloves and got the car out.

As I drove along the coast road, the mist got thinner, though there was still enough to obscure the view across the Bristol Channel on one side and the high moorland on the other. I drove down Countisbury Hill into Lynmouth (empty now of tourists and only the gulls and the jackdaws inhabiting the seafront), and up again into Lynton and then on towards the Valley of Rocks, but turning left back onto the moor again until I finally found the large, imposing building that was St. Winifred's Home. It stood in solitary splendor, its Victorian Gothic towers overlooking lawns and shrubberies that, though they were doubtless pleasant in summer, now had a dismal appearance. There was no one about — not surprising, I suppose, in view of the weather, but nonetheless adding to my feeling of unreality, and it was with some relief that I saw a prosaic sign saying VISITORS' PARKING. Grateful for this sign of normality, I drove the car into the space indicated and got out.

There was a heavy, complicated lock on the massive front door and at one side a modern bell commanding one to RING AND WAIT. After a while, through the stained-glass panel (the ecclesiastical theme?) in the door I saw a figure in a green overall who unlocked it and, inviting me in, locked it behind me. Noticing my startled look, she said, "We have to keep it locked, you understand. Some of the old dears go walkabout if we don't." She was a pleasant, middle-aged woman with a strong Welsh accent, and she ushered me into a small waiting room. "Who was it you were wanting to see, dear?" she asked.

I almost asked for Sybil, but remembered just in time that now she had another name, and I must get used to calling her by it.

"Sister Veronica, please; she is expecting me."

"Right you are, dear. I'll just go and see if I can find her."

The waiting room was rather dark, with one small window (more stained glass), and was furnished only with a table with four upright chairs standing stiffly around it. There were several magazines on the table, and I picked one up, expecting it to be of some religious nature, but it was an old copy of *What Car,* and the others were equally unexpected — *Woman's Own, Country Living* and *Hello* magazine. Encouraged by the secular nature of the reading matter provided, I sat down and picked up the latter. I was absorbed in pictures of the wedding of two American film stars I'd never heard of, when the door opened and Sybil — that is, Veronica — came in.

She was wearing the sort of dress (one could hardly call it a habit) that Mrs. Dudley had described and, indeed, she did look like an old-fashioned nanny. She came forward into the room with her hand outstretched.

"Sheila, this is a pleasure. Do forgive me for keeping you waiting, but I was in the laundry." She smiled, seeing my puzzled expression. "All our residents are elderly, so, as you can imagine, keeping up with the laundry is an ongoing problem."

"Of course," I said.

"Well, now," Veronica continued, "let's go up to my room, where we can have a proper chat."

She led the way through the hall, up a fine, ornately carved staircase, and along a series of corridors, each lined with heavy doors with little brass slots, like those in Victorian pews, marked with their occupants' names. Like all residential homes, it was very warm, but today, given the miserable weather outside, the warmth was welcome. Veronica's room was quite small and at the back of the house with a view over part of the vegetable garden. There was a divan bed with a cream candlewick cover along one wall, a small bedside table, a table with one upright chair, and two armchairs facing the window. The curtains at the tall window were brocade, faded to some indeterminate color, and the carpet was a neutral green. The room was saved from dullness by the fact that the walls were lined with bookshelves crammed with books, many still in their bright jackets, and the presence of a large, white cyclamen plant on the table.

"Do sit down," Veronica said. "I've asked Gwyneth to bring some coffee."

"That would be lovely," I said. Then, uncertain of what to say next, I went on, "It's so nice to see you again — I can't remember when the last time was."

"A funeral, I expect," Veronica said with a smile. "It usually is." She indicated the armchairs. "Do sit down."

There was a knock on the door and the woman in the green overall came in with a tray with two cups of coffee, a bowl of sugar and a plate with four plain biscuits on it.

"There you are, Sister," she said. "Sorry about the biscuits, but Mrs. Granger had the last of the shortbreads." She put the tray down on the table and went away.

Veronica handed me one of the cups of coffee and I refused the sugar and the biscuits. We sat in silence for a moment; then she said, "It's always lovely to see you, Sheila, but do I get the feeling there's a reason for this particular visit?"

I nodded. "Actually, yes there is." I put my coffee cup back on the table. "Do you remember a cousin of ours, Bernard Prior?

He was down here doing genealogical research into the Priors, and he's been calling on members of the family, asking for photos, documents and so on. I wondered if he'd been to see you."

I became aware of the fact that Veronica was sitting very still, almost holding her breath. She didn't reply straightaway, but then she said in a calm, measured voice, "Yes, I remember Bernard Prior, and no, he didn't call on me."

I looked at her curiously, but her face was impassive.

"Oh, well . . . it's just that I thought I'd better let you know — he's dead."

"Dead?" Her voice was no longer calm. "Dead? Do you mean that?" she asked urgently. "Really dead?"

"Well — yes, really dead." I said.

"Thank God," she said.

This reaction disconcerted me so much that I simply didn't know what to say, so I remained silent.

"Thank God," she repeated and got up and went over to the window where she stood for some minutes looking out. Then she turned and came slowly back and sat down again, gripping the arms of the chair tightly. She was very pale and she took deep breaths as if to restore her composure.

"Are you all right?" I asked anxiously and made a movement to get up. "Shall I call someone?"

"No, no . . ." She made a great effort to speak. "It was a shock — I'll be all right; just give me a minute."

I sat quietly for what seemed like a long time, though it was probably only a few minutes, and then Veronica said, "I'm so sorry. You must wonder what on earth —" She broke off and got up again, this time pacing up and down the room. "I've tried so hard, you see, prayed so much, but I couldn't — I *couldn't* forgive him. Even now, you see, even now when he's dead. You'd think that *now* . . ." She made a despairing gesture and stood quite still. After a moment she seemed to collect herself and came back and sat down. She took a deep breath.

"I'm sorry, Sheila. You must think I'm completely mad. Perhaps I am, where that man is concerned. When did he die, and how?"

I told her what had happened and for a moment she said nothing. Then she gave a wry smile. "So there was someone else who hated him as much as I did," she said. "What a pity he was already dead and they didn't know it."

She saw my expression and shook her

head. "I know, I know. It's a shocking thing to say, especially by someone in my position, and, as I said, I've tried to forgive him for the awful things he did, and, indeed, I'll go on trying for the rest of my life. Then perhaps *my* trespasses may be forgiven. It is, after all, a fundamental tenet of Christianity, is it not?" She smiled. "I suppose I should tell you what on earth all this is about."

"No, really, you don't have to," I said, "not if it upsets you."

"I think you deserve an explanation after my little outburst just now. I'm sorry to have inflicted that on you, but, well, it was, as I said, a shock."

"If you're sure."

She nodded. "You remember Alma, my younger sister? She married someone called Howard Osborne, a nice man but not strong — he'd had tuberculosis when he was young, and it left him with a weakness so he couldn't work full-time. He was a part-time library assistant, but of course, that didn't bring in much money, so Alma trained as a nurse, and when their son, Robin, was born, she went to work for an agency so that she could arrange her shifts to look after him." She smiled reminiscently. "Robin was a lovely boy, so sweet natured, a bit delicate, though — they had worries about him, worries about his lungs, of course — and perhaps, being an only child, a bit timid and introverted, but such a happy child. They were all so happy. I used to go and stay with them sometimes, and the atmosphere in that household was so warm and loving —" She broke off and sat in silence for a moment. "When Robin was about twelve, Alma ran into Bernard Prior — I think he had to come to the hospital for something; anyway, they met again. We'd both known Bernard when we were children; we used to be invited round to tea with him — he was an only child and his mother (such a nice woman) worried that he didn't have enough company of children of his own age and he didn't seem to have any friends. We never liked him because he was what we called 'bossy,' but I suppose it was really bullying. But you know how it is; if your parents arrange things, you don't really feel you can do anything about it. Well, that's how we used to feel — I expect children today speak up for themselves more than we did."

"Indeed they do!" I said.

Veronica acknowledged my interjection with a smile and went on. "Anyway, Bernard seemed quite pleased to see Alma, went on about the old days and so forth, and invited them all to Sunday lunch, so they went. After that they saw quite a bit of Bernard and his family. Alma didn't really want to — she found Bernard as domineering as he used to be and was so sorry for his poor wife and children, especially the boy — but, as she said, it was difficult to keep on finding excuses without sounding rude.

"Bernard had just been made headmaster at this private school and, when Robin was thirteen, he suggested to Alma and Howard that he should become a pupil there. Of course, Alma said they couldn't possibly afford the fees, but Bernard said that he'd waive the fees because Robin was such a bright boy, he deserved the best chance they could give him."

"That was generous."

Veronica shook her head. "Bernard never did anything without an ulterior motive."

"I can imagine," I said.

"Robin really was bright and was obviously going to do well in exams, and with league tables being as important as they are, I can see that Bernard thought he'd be useful."

"Oh, those wretched league tables! They seem to be the be-all and end-all of everything now!"

"Well, Alma and Howard talked it over and decided that they ought to accept Bernard's offer. His school had a very good academic reputation and could give Robin a lot of things his local comprehensive couldn't. So they said thank you very much and Robin started at the beginning of the next term." Veronica paused for a moment, as if remembering something, then went on. "It was all fine to begin with. Robin did very well and his teachers were pleased with him, and the other boys seemed friendly enough, but after a while things started to go wrong. I think I told you that Robin was rather a timid child, overprotected, I suppose — he was so precious to them — and I suppose that sort of child does tend to attract the bullies, and that is what happened. It wasn't bad at first, just a bit of name-calling, but when they saw he was scared, it got worse. Then one of them found out his parents didn't pay any fees and they taunted him about that, and it was made worse when they discovered Bernard was a relation."

"Children can be very cruel," I said.

"It wasn't just the children," Veronica said. "Bernard began to ask Robin about the other pupils — who was doing something wrong, who was responsible for various things that had happened in the school — making him a spy, in fact."

"But that's awful!"

"Of course Robin didn't want to, but Bernard told him that it was the least he could do, because his parents didn't pay."

"No! He actually *said* that?"

"Not in so many words, of course, but he implied it. 'Your parents would be so grieved to know how ungrateful you are being' — that sort of thing. Robin was totally confused; he adored his parents and couldn't bear the thought of upsetting them, so he did what Bernard asked."

"The poor child!"

"It wasn't long before the bullies found out, and then it really was hell for him. The ringleader was a boy called Desmond, and the rest of the gang kowtowed to him because he was the son of the local millionaire. Anyway, this boy decided that the best way to teach Robin a lesson, as he called it, was to introduce him to drugs."

"Good heavens."

"The group had been smoking cannabis — I imagine it was quite easy to get if you had the money. So instead of tormenting Robin, this Desmond said he knew the sneaking wasn't his fault and he could join the gang. Again, I don't think Robin wanted to, but anything was better than the misery he'd been enduring. They said he had to smoke the cannabis if he wanted to be part of the group, and so he did."

"What about his parents? Didn't he tell them what was happening?"

Veronica shook her head. "No. Howard wasn't well and his mother was working all the hours she could just to keep their heads above water financially. Poor Robin didn't want to give them any more worries, so he kept all this to himself. And I was too far away down here for him to be able to turn to me. If only I'd known . . ."

Her voice trailed away and she took a few moments to recover.

"Things went from bad to worse. They made Robin collect the stuff from the dealer, and by then it was hard drugs, not just cannabis, and the inevitable happened: he was caught by the police."

"Did Bernard have any idea of what had been going on?"

"I'm not sure, but he may have done. The fact is, though, when this Desmond swore that he had nothing to do with it and said Robin was the ringleader, Bernard backed him up."

"What!"

"Desmond's father was rich and influential; Robin was the perfect scapegoat." She paused for a while and then went on. "I think the police suspected the truth, but there was no evidence against Desmond, and Robin had been caught red-handed, as it were, and however much he protested his innocence, there was nothing he could do. But the police did try to make things easier for him. He wasn't sent to a young offenders' center, thank God, and just did community service. But he has a police record."

"What happened at the school?"

"Oh, Bernard expelled him with a great deal of fuss and commotion. You know — 'An example must be made to show we won't tolerate such behavior,' and, of course, 'After all I've done for this boy' — that sort of thing."

"How awful for Alma."

"She and Howard were devastated. Of course they believed Robin, but there was nothing they could do. Still, that wasn't the worst problem. The awful fact was that Robin had become an addict. They got him into a rehab program and for a while they thought things were going to be all right. But he lapsed. Time and again he's lapsed, and now — well . . ."

"That is really terrible."

"It completely overwhelmed poor

Howard. The worry and the sheer awfulness of what had happened were simply too much for someone in such frail health. He died a year after, and ever since, Alma has been trying to keep some sort of home together for herself and Robin and trying desperately to keep him clean."

She finished speaking and we sat there in silence for some time. Veronica looked drained and tired, as if she couldn't talk anymore, and I was so overwhelmed by the dreadful story she'd just told me that I couldn't find any words to speak of it. After a while she got up and went over to the window. Looking out, with her back to me she said, "So you see why Bernard Prior was unlikely to call on me, and why I thank God that he is dead." She turned and faced me. "No, I didn't kill him, though I have often wished to, may God forgive me. And Alma didn't kill him either. For the last two months she's been up in Newcastle, finding work where she can, trying, once again, to support Robin on yet another rehab program."

CHAPTER SEVENTEEN

When I drove away, the mist had lifted but the sky was still iron gray and the whole landscape seemed drained of light. Somehow I didn't want to go straight home. I needed time to take in the dreadful things Veronica had told me, so I took the long way back, over the moor, and stopped in a layby to collect my thoughts. The feelings she'd described were so strong, the events so vivid, that I felt I'd somehow been living them with her and I needed time to come back to my own world.

I watched the sheep moving down the slope into the combe below, nibbling the short grass as they went, saw the crows wheeling overhead and heard the cry of a seagull perched on a mound covered with dead heather, hoping for some titbit from my parked car. Slowly I began to understand fully the horror of what had happened to that family, and the extent of Bernard's responsibility for it. More than ever, when I thought of the irreparable damage he'd done to so many people, I felt, with Veronica, glad that he was dead. The heart attack was, perhaps, divine justice — was that how Veronica thought of it? I wondered. But if only it had remained a natural death; if only that blow had not been struck. Admittedly, if what Roger and Michael had told me was true, then no one could be prosecuted for the attack, but all the same I couldn't leave it alone, I still needed to know who had tried to kill him.

Veronica said she hadn't done it (and her reaction to the news of his death made me feel that she was telling the truth), and Alma and Robin were far away, so there seemed to be no one left. No one in the family, that is. I suddenly remembered the conversation I'd had with Raymond Poyser about the boy — his neighbor's nephew — at Bernard's school who'd tried to commit suicide. That had been about bullying too. His parents would have felt as badly as Veronica and Alma; would, surely, have wanted Bernard dead. I sat thinking about this while the rain began to fall, that sort of fine, wetting rain, whipped up by the wind that almost always cuts across the high moor, sweeping it in waves so that it almost obliterated the landscape in front of me.

It wouldn't do, I decided eventually. How would they have known that Bernard was down here in Taviscombe? It would obviously have been easier to kill him in Bristol. And, anyway, why wait so long after the event? No, I decided regretfully, although they certainly had a motive, it was unlikely that the parents of that poor boy could have killed the man they knew was responsible for their son's desperate act.

So I was back to the family again, and the feeling I'd had all along that Bernard's own research had been responsible for what had happened. But there was no one left.

"Yes there is!" I said aloud, startling myself with the sound of my own voice in the enclosed confines of the car. "There's Fred!"

I suppose I'd forgotten about Fred because he lived in Bristol and not locally, but there was no reason to think that Bernard hadn't been in touch with him too and that he'd mentioned his projected trip to Taviscombe. Surely there'd been notes attached to Fred's family tree. I couldn't remember. I started the car and began the journey home, anxious to see what, if anything, Bernard had discovered about that particular branch of the family and whether there was something there that might conceivably have provided a motive for murder.

But, of course, I couldn't get out the papers and start looking straightaway. The animals, resentful at my absence, persecuted me unmercifully, gulping down their food and then asking (vociferously) to go out, and then, when they saw that it was still raining (at every door), asking for more food, and, when that was gone, demanding my undivided attention. When I'd finally got them settled (putting an extra bar of the electric fire on in the sitting room and bribing them with handfuls of dried food, which I knew they'd scatter far and wide, so that I'd be vacuuming it up for days) and I was just about to get out the briefcase with the papers in it, the telephone rang. It was Janet, asking whether I'd had the notice about going to the inquest on Bernard's death. Mine had arrived a few days ago and I'd pushed it to the back of my mind and almost forgotten it.

"Yes," I said. "I assumed they'd want you there too, but I wasn't sure if you'd be well enough to come."

"Oh, yes, I'm fine now. My arm's still strapped up, though, so I can't drive, but Christine insists on coming too." There was a slight undertone of irritation in her voice. "So she'll bring me."

"Let me see, now; it's at eleven o'clock. Will you both come back here for lunch?"

"That's very kind of you, but I think Christine wants to get straight back to Bristol — some important meeting she needs to go to."

"What a pity, it would have been nice to have a chat."

"Actually, the other reason I rang was to see if you're still all right about coming to the funeral. We — that is, Christine has arranged it for Friday. It's eleven thirty at the crematorium and then back here afterwards. I do so hope you can come; it would mean a lot to me."

"Yes, of course I will."

"Luke won't be there of course . . . well, it would hardly be — well — suitable, really. So I'd be glad of your support."

"No, that's fine. I'll be there."

"The crematorium is at Canford; that's Westbury on Trim. Can you find it?"

"That's all right. I know where it is."

"Oh, good." Janet paused for a minute; then she said tentatively, "I wonder if you'd feel like staying the night. To save you the journey back the same day. And," she added "it would be so nice to have that chat."

"That's very kind of you, but I really don't think I can leave the animals. But I'll stay on afterwards and we can talk then."

"Oh, good. Well, I'll see you at the inquest, then. I do hope it won't be too awful — I'm really dreading it."

"No, I think it'll be quite straightforward — at least that's what I gathered from Roger — just explaining how we . . . how we found Bernard. That sort of thing."

"Well," Janet said, "I won't feel so bad if you're there too."

The inquest was, as Roger had said, really only a matter of form. The coroner did refer to "some unusual circumstances" but didn't go into any sort of detail and pronounced the death to be "from natural causes." I was pleased to see that the young man who does the court cases for the local paper didn't seem to be there, so I hoped that the whole business would escape notice in the press. Janet had made her statement after me. She spoke in a low voice but seemed to be quite calm, although I thought Christine looked rather nervous while she was speaking. Afterwards I hardly had time to have a word, before Christine, with a brief, perfunctory apology, took her away again.

"I'll see you on Friday," Janet said as

Christine shut the car door.

I waved them off and stood for a moment outside the rather dismal redbrick building that housed the magistrates court and the police station, trying to take in the fact that it was all over.

"So that's that, then." Sergeant Harris came out of the court and joined me. "Funny sort of business altogether," he said.

"It certainly was," I replied. "So that's it, is it?"

"Well, of course, there's still some paper-work to do — but, then, when isn't there!"

"But you won't be investigating anything else?"

"Like the coroner said, it was death from natural causes. There is the question of the break-in, but, honestly, Mrs. Malory, since nothing seems to have been stolen, I don't think there's much we can do about it now."

"No, of course not. Well, it will be a great relief to Mrs. Prior to have it all over."

"Yes, poor lady, it must have been a dread-ful experience for her — well, you too, if it comes to that, finding him like that — but she seems to be the sort of lady who would be easily upset, if you know what I mean."

I agreed with his estimate of Janet's character and thought ruefully that I obvi-ously didn't give the impression of equal sensitivity.

He moved towards the door of the police station. "I'd better be getting along," he said. "Like I said — all that paperwork."

" 'A policeman's lot is not a happy one,' " I quoted. He looked at me blankly and I hastily added, "Gilbert and Sullivan, *Pirates of Penzance.*"

His face cleared. "That's right," he said. "The wife and I went to see it in Taunton last year." He hummed a few bars. "A really good evening out! Oh, well, back to my *constabulary duties,*" he said with a jovial emphasis, and went in.

I thought a little sea air would dispel the depressing atmosphere of the inquest, so I drove down to the harbor and stood for a while watching the sea. A little way out, a determined (or perhaps foolish) sailboarder was battling with a stiff breeze, sometimes making good progress towards the shore; then the sail would tip over and he'd be in the sea, and I watched anxiously as he scrambled back onto the board again. Time and again it happened: just as he seemed to be all set for the beach, the wind would upset him and he was struggling in the water again. A bit like my "investigations," I thought. A lot of effort leading nowhere. Oh, well, it was all over now. The case (such as it was) was closed and it really didn't matter (did it?) who had struck that blow. I could put it out of my mind. But as I stood there watching the sailboarder, I knew that I'd go on (determined or foolish), like him, not because I *had* to, but for my own satisfaction. And, as I watched, he finally made it to the shore and stood for a triumphant moment, looking out at the sea he'd emerged from, before making his way cautiously across the stony beach, back to his car.

Because I'm not very good at finding my way anywhere, I always leave plenty of time, so I was very early at the crematorium on the Friday morning. I found a good parking place not too far from the entrance and sat quietly for a while listening to some nice, soothing Elgar on the car radio. Gradually the other mourners began to arrive, mostly middle-aged, colleagues perhaps. As far as I could see, there were no other relatives, though, given the circumstances, that was not surprising. About ten minutes before the service was to begin I got out of the car and went in.

Like all crematoriums, this one was bright and airy, with a great deal of light wood everywhere in both fittings and furnishings.

There were several large and impressive flower arrangements, designed, perhaps, to draw attention away from the curtains behind a kind of altar, though, of course, one's eye was inevitably, if reluctantly, focused upon them. There was a lectern with a microphone, and what appeared to be recorded music permeated the whole space — a careful combination of the religious and the secular, an attempt to be all things to all men, as it were, trying to offend no one, even if, in the end, no one was truly satisfied.

The service itself was a little like the crematorium — parts of the Prayer Book service interspersed with readings and two brief eulogies (praising Bernard's "dedication to education"). People bent over their orders of service trying to keep up, joining in thankfully, back on safe ground, with the Lord's Prayer. The service proceeded to its ineluctable end, and we all queued up to shake hands with Janet, Christine and a tall thin man in spectacles whom I took to be Christine's husband.

"A very nice service." I murmured the conventional words as I greeted Janet.

"You can find your way back to the house?" she said anxiously.

"Yes, of course."

"I'm so glad you came —"

Christine interrupted. "Dr. Fenchurch, Mother," she said, indicating an elderly gentleman who had come up behind me. "You remember he was so helpful to Father about those census reports."

"So good of you to come," Janet said dutifully, as quiet and subdued as the old Janet had been, and I moved on, out into the fresh air and back into the outside world. As I was standing beside my car, an elderly man came up to me.

"Sheila? It's been a long time, but you look so like your father I knew I couldn't be mistaken." It was Fred Prior.

"Fred, how nice to see you! I didn't see you at the service."

"No, I always sit at the back at these affairs, in case I want to make an unobtrusive getaway." He gave me a quick smile. "I didn't know you were a friend of the late lamented."

"Not a friend," I said, "but I wanted to be here for Janet."

"Ah, poor Janet. Freedom at last, eh?"

"Well, yes," I said, a little disconcerted at his forthright remarks, though I did remember that Fred had always had the reputation (carefully fostered by himself) of being eccentric.

"Are you *going back?*" he asked, giving the words an ironic emphasis.

"Yes, I promised Janet that I would. How about you?"

"No fear. Not my scene at all. I only came to see old Bernard off."

"Oh, right . . ."

"It would have been nice to have had a word with you. I always liked your father, and your mother was one of the wittiest women I've ever known. Next time you're coming to Bristol, give me a ring and we'll have lunch." He looked round. "They're all coming out now, so I'll make my escape. Don't forget; give me a ring." He gave a wave and got into a dashing Mercedes sports car that I'd been admiring in the parking lot and drove off.

Bernard's house — and I'm sure it was always Bernard's house and not Janet's — was on a quiet, leafy road in a pleasant suburb of Bristol near Clifton and the Downs. It was a tall, Edwardian, three-story building set well back from the road with a lot of shrubs in front of it and a substantial driveway. There were already several cars parked there when I arrived (having got lost in one of the city's difficult one-way systems), so I left my car in the road so that I could get out easily if it all became too much for me.

Although there had been a fair number of people at the service, there were only about a dozen at the house. Mostly, as I had suspected, former colleagues, including the two who had read the eulogies. One of these, a large, bald man with glasses, was holding forth in a loud, pompous manner about the problems of modern education with reference to the total failure of the comprehensive system. This was obviously a familiar theme, and the eyes of his listeners had glazed over as they stood there balancing glasses of red wine and plates with vol-au-vents and small triangular sandwiches. My entrance obviously provided a welcome opportunity for them to break out of the circle surrounding him and re-form into small groups, where they engaged in hastily improvised conversations of their own.

Christine, who had let me in, took me around, introducing me ("This is Sheila Prior, my father's cousin") to the various people. The names, of course, meant nothing to me, or mine to them, and, burdened in my turn with plate and glass, I stood uncomfortably making the sort of small talk one does on such occasions. It became apparent, as I spoke to various people, that the more bizarre aspect of Bernard's death had not been made public, since everyone made some reference to the heart attack, expressing surprise ("Never knew Bernard had a heart condition. Just goes to show . . ."), but I imagine Christine wouldn't have wanted anything that might have been regarded as scandalous connected with her father, or, indeed, herself, and I didn't think that Janet would have had any say in the matter.

Escaping from the tedious proceedings for a moment, I went over to the table by the window to put my glass down.

"Hello. I don't think we've been introduced. I'm Jonathan Taylor, Christine's husband."

I turned and saw the tall man who'd been standing by Christine at the service holding out his hand.

"How do you do," I replied formally and went on to make some trite remark about it being a sad occasion.

"Yes, indeed," he said in a way that suggested that he was used to agreeing with whomever he happened to be speaking to.

"Christine has organized everything quite splendidly," I said. "Janet must be very pleased to have it all done so well. It's always such a difficult time."

"Yes, indeed," he said again, adding after

a pause, "Christine's very good at organizing things."

"She was most efficient down at Taviscombe when her father — died." I wasn't sure how much even Christine's husband had been allowed to know. "Things were quite complicated and she was most helpful."

He smiled politely but made no comment, possibly because just then Christine came up to us, saying, "Jonathan, Mr. Purvis is going now," and led him away.

Gradually the other guests left and, finally, Christine, with admonitions to her mother to leave all the clearing up to the caterers ("who will be calling at five"), took her husband away, and Janet and I were left alone.

Chapter Eighteen

"Goodness," Janet said. "I thought they'd never go. Would you like a glass of wine?"

"No. thanks; I've got to drive home. A cup of tea would be nice, though."

"Good idea. Let's go into the kitchen."

The kitchen was expensively fitted with dark, solid-looking wooden units, which were a bit overpowering, but Janet indicated a pleasant space, near the French doors looking out onto the garden, with a table and four chairs. "Do sit down and I'll put the kettle on."

I was struck, as I had been before, at the way she could change suddenly from a dispirited, downtrodden victim to a cheerful, lively human being.

"The service went very well," I said. "Christine organized everything splendidly."

"Yes, she's been much more herself lately. Just before Bernard died she was very down about something."

"Really?"

She brought the tea tray over to the table and sat down.

"I think it's Jonathan," she said. "Her husband. Did you meet him?"

"Very briefly. We were about to embark on a conversation — I think. He seemed very shy — but then Christine took him away."

"That sounds about right," Janet said. "He is a bit of a cipher; I suppose that's why Christine married him. Inoffensive and always there — a bit like me and Bernard, I suppose." I looked at her in surprise and she smiled. "Well I'd have been a *total* fool if I hadn't worked that one out."

The kettle was making bubbling noises and she went over and made the tea.

"If he's so innocuous," I said, "then why should Christine be worried about him?"

"Money. It usually is with Christine. He's been making some rather foolish investments that have gone wrong. The stupid boy — he thought that if he could show Christine he could make a fair amount of money, then she'd respect him more."

"Oh, dear. And it's gone wrong?"

"Badly wrong, I'm afraid."

"How did you find out?"

"He talks to me sometimes — fellow feeling, I suppose — and he had to tell someone about it. Anyway, he didn't just lose his investment, he's also got himself quite badly into debt."

"And Christine doesn't know?"

"Oh, yes, I'm pretty sure she found out, though, of course, she'd never tell me — she couldn't bear me to know that things weren't perfect in every aspect of her life." She sighed. "The trouble is, they're very overextended financially. Christine does like to make a show — you know, big house, big car (two cars, actually), expensive social life, that sort of lifestyle."

"Oh, dear."

"I did wonder if she'd approached Bernard for help, but, again, I don't think she could bear him to know what sort of mess Jonathan had made of things. Bernard never liked him, always thought Christine could have done better for herself, although he rather liked the idea of Jonathan's family."

"His family?"

"His father was an admiral and his mother belongs to an old county family — Bernard was a terrible snob."

"Oh, I see. Poor Jonathan. He looked rather pleasant."

"He is. I'm very fond of him. He should have married a nice, quiet girl who would have looked up to him, but I suppose he was attracted by Christine's self-assurance, or something."

"She's very good-looking," I said. "That dark hair and blue eyes are very striking."

"Yes. She takes after my father; everyone said he was a very handsome man." She was silent for a moment. "I can only just remember him. He was in the army — he was killed when I was five."

"I'm so sorry," I said. I wondered whether Janet had married Bernard because she was looking for a father figure. *Not* a good idea. "So you think," I continued, "that Christine was worried about money?"

"I'm pretty sure that was it." She suddenly remembered the tea and poured us each a cup. "Still," she went on, "she'll be all right now."

"Really?"

"Oh, yes. Bernard's will."

I looked at her inquiringly.

"Bernard arranged that I should have a small proportion of his pension if he died before me — though I'm sure he imagined he'd outlive me — and he's left me the house, but everything else goes to Christine. There's quite a bit: he made some very good investments and he was always very careful with money."

"That seems unfair."

She shrugged. "Well, she was the only person he really cared about; I suppose it was to be expected."

"Still . . ."

"Oh, I don't mind. I expect the house will fetch quite a lot. Some developer will turn it into flats; there's plenty of room for that."

"So you won't go on living here."

She gave a barely perceptible shudder. "No. I couldn't. Too many unhappy memories, and, anyway, it's far too big. It was too big for Bernard and me, but, of course, he wouldn't move — it was part of his image of himself, I suppose."

"Well, I'm sure you're right and it will fetch a good price. Where will you live?"

She smiled happily. "With Luke and Yves, of course. I can use the money from the house for them to get somewhere really good, a better position for the restaurant. It will be wonderful."

"Have you told Christine yet?"

She shook her head. "I'll wait until I have to. Try to catch her in a good mood. Still," she went on, an unaccustomed note of defiance in her voice, "she can't stop me. Especially if I've got Luke and Yves to back me up. I'll wait until I've sold the house. Though I expect she'll want to do *that* as well."

I thought that was highly probable, since I couldn't imagine Christine would think her mother capable of doing something so important on her own.

"You could say your solicitor was advising you," I suggested.

"Oh, no, he'd be on Christine's side. He was a friend of Bernard and he's Christine's godfather. So I certainly won't let him know what I'm doing. No, I'll leave it to Luke. He's very capable, you know," she said, her face lighting up as it always did when she spoke of him. "You have to be really practical to run a successful restaurant, and Yves is marvelous at bargaining — the French, you know, always so good with money!"

"Well," I said, "I do hope everything turns out splendidly for you and Luke."

She went on for a bit about his plans for the new restaurant, but I was only half listening, wondering when, if ever, she would refer to the circumstances of Bernard's death. But when it was time for me to go, she still hadn't mentioned it and I felt a certain reluctance to do so, given the occasion. I did ask whether Bernard had ever expressed any wish about having his ashes scattered somewhere in particular.

"No," she said, "he never said anything about things like that — I suppose he thought he'd go on forever. Christine thought it would be nice if they were scattered at his school, but they weren't very keen about that — not surprising, if you think about it — so I expect it will just be here in the garden. Christine will see to it."

I was slightly shocked at her tone and attitude until I remembered just what sort of life she had led with Bernard.

"Well," I said, getting up, "I must get off. Do let me know how things go."

She gave me a hug and said, "Thank you so much for coming, Sheila — it was so nice to know that I had one friend here. And — well — thank you for everything."

It was getting dark as I set off, and starting to rain, and because of that, the traffic on the M5, bad at the best of times, was really awful, so that I had to concentrate hard on my driving and couldn't go over in my mind the incidents of the day. Only when I'd left the motorway and the traffic jams in Bridgwater behind me did I have an opportunity to think about what had happened. One phrase stuck in my mind: Janet had called me her friend. But I wasn't — I was really sorry for her, of course, and interested in her plans in the way that I was interested in the characters and the plot of a soap opera, but it occurred to me that it wouldn't worry me if I never saw her or heard from her again. No, not really a friend. I would hear from her again, I was pretty sure of that; she would want to "keep in touch." Oh, well. I could manage that.

I was really tired when I got to the out-skirts of Taviscombe so I got myself some fish and chips (extra fish to propitiate the animals) to save cooking. Later in the evening, when I was able to relax at last, I thought over the events of the day in more detail. As Janet had said, it wasn't surprising that, having made some sort of basic provision for her, Bernard had left everything to Christine. Interesting that Christine was worried about money — though typical, I felt, that the problem should not have been of her own making. I had a moment of sympathy for poor Jonathan, since I could imagine only too well the contempt with which his wife would be treating him after his unfortunate financial dealings. Money problems would be intolerable to Christine. How lucky, therefore, that she now had the means to put things right and even increase her comfortable lifestyle. Lucky, indeed, that her father died when he did. It was, when you came to think of it, a possible motive for murder.

To clear my head I picked up my tray and

carried it out to the kitchen. Foss, ever on the lookout for extra rations, followed me, though Tris, surfeited with battered cod, remained supine in front of the electric fire. I scraped the bits of batter from my plate into Foss's dish and began to wash up my supper things. Money was always a substantial motive for murder; Roger often said so. And I was sure that Christine would have had the resolution to do it. Of course, there was the fact that she was her father's favorite and was said to have been fond of him, but it was just possible that her passionate desire to maintain and improve her position might have been sufficient to overcome any qualms she might have about disposing of him.

But there was another fact, and one that made me reluctantly abandon my theory. She had a perfectly good alibi. Luke had telephoned her that night — at home in Bristol, and at a time when it would have been impossible for her to have traveled to Taviscombe to do the deed. There was no reason for Luke, who had no cause to like his sister, to lie for her. So she simply couldn't have done it. Which was a pity, since she was such an unpleasant person that she would have made an acceptable suspect. For a moment I considered the possibility that Jonathan had been dispatched to eliminate his father-in-law, but a moment's thought made me realize how impossible that would have been. Even if he'd been capable of such a thing (which he palpably wasn't), there's no way Christine would have trusted him with something so important. With a sigh, I tipped away the washing-up water and abandoned my theories.

The next morning Michael called in on his way to work. The lightbulb on the landing had gone, and I couldn't reach it to put in a new one. For years I've been meaning to have the light fitting moved, but somehow I've never got round to it. I stood on the landing, peering anxiously up at Michael as he leaned precariously over the banisters to put the new bulb in.

"Thank you so much, darling," I said. "I'm so sorry to bother you."

"No trouble. Anyway, the bulb up here only goes *phut* once every couple of years."

I followed him downstairs and he stopped at the bottom.

"Ma," he said, "you really must get some new stair carpet; look at the state of it!"

The carpet certainly was pretty bad, worn thin in places and elsewhere reduced to a sort of loosely looped bouclé.

"I know it looks awful, but, honestly,

there's no point in renewing it. Foss will only claw the new one to pieces."

"That's as may be, but it really isn't safe. Look, there are actual *holes* in it in places. No, really," he said firmly, "you must do something about it."

"All right, darling, I'll go to the carpet place today; I promise. Now, then, have you got time for a cup of coffee?"

"No, thanks. I must be off. I've got a nine thirty appointment. Don't forget about that stair carpet!"

A little later in the morning, when I found Foss at the top of the stairs, busily clawing away, I looked more carefully at the carpet and decided that Michael was right. So I went down to see Mr. Davis at the furniture and carpet shop, explaining that I wanted something *very* hard wearing. He pointed me in the direction of various carpet samples and I was busy studying them when Anthea suddenly materialized behind me.

"Ah, Sheila — so glad I bumped into you; I was going to ring you. We need a steward for Brunswick Lodge next Wednesday. Mary Thomas has got the appointment for her knee replacement at last, so we need someone to cover for her. Can you do it?"

I really didn't feel like standing about all morning at Brunswick Lodge, so I decided that only a downright lie would do.

"I'm so sorry, but I can't manage that."

"Oh?" Anthea is not used to people not falling in with her plans. "Why not?"

"Um." I thought quickly. "I've got to go to Bristol that day."

"Oh, well." Anything away from Taviscombe is recognized to fall outside Anthea's jurisdiction. She regarded the carpet samples I'd been looking at with a jaundiced eye. "It's no good buying anything that isn't pure wool," she said. "A false economy in the long run."

"I just want something that's resistant to cats' claws," I said hopelessly.

"Oh, well, if you will insist on filling your house with *animals*," she said as she moved away.

I chose something that looked as if it might stand up to a feline assault and went in search of Mr. Davis.

"Right you are, Mrs. Malory. I'll order it right away — shouldn't take too long to come through. I can't send Denzil round to measure up until the end of next week. One of our busiest times of the year, everyone wanting things for Christmas." He noticed my air of bewilderment (why would people want to celebrate a Christian festival by ordering soft furnishings?). "Christmas holidays — friends and family coming to stay."

"Of course," I said. "No, the end of next week will be fine."

"That's good, then. Denzil will give you a ring about the time."

I had intended to go home for lunch but I ran into Rosemary, who inveigled me into having a sandwich at the Buttery.

"Mother's driving me absolutely mad about this ruby wedding thing," she said, picking the cucumber out of her ham and salad sandwich. "I do so love cucumber, but I really daren't risk it. Anyway, she's *still* going on about a grand dinner at the Castle in Taunton — apparently Jocelyn Forsyth's daughter had her silver wedding 'do' there and, you know what Mother's like; she can't bear to be upstaged by one of her friends."

"You'll have to give in, in the end," I said. "She always wins."

"No," Rosemary said firmly. "This time I'm not letting her tell me what to do. I said to Jack, even if it means we have to get *divorced* I'm not going to do it!"

I laughed. "And what did Jack say?"

"Oh, you know what he's like. He just said everything would be fine and went and shut himself in his study. Men!"

"You'll think of something," I said soothingly. "Just book somewhere and present her with a fait accompli."

"I suppose so," Rosemary said reluctantly, "but it's not what I really want."

"What do you want?"

She laughed. "That's it — I don't know! Something different, I suppose, but I don't know what. Still, that's enough of my troubles. How did you get on at the funeral?"

I told her all about it, and then I said, "I know it should have been a sort of — what's the word? — closure, but somehow it wasn't. I still feel there are all sorts of loose ends."

"Well, *you* don't have to tidy them up."

"No, I suppose not, but it's irritating somehow."

When I got home I decided to vacuum the sitting room and, as I was moving the furniture, I came across Bernard's briefcase, which I'd put down behind the table. I remembered that I'd meant to see what research Bernard had made into Fred's family, so I unplugged the Hoover, put it away, sat down at the table, and opened the briefcase. After shuffling through a lot of stuff, I finally found Fred's family tree and saw that there were indeed some notes paper clipped to it. I read them and then looked carefully at the family tree and decided that there was something there that, although not really a motive for murder, was certainly worth considering. Certainly worth taking up Fred's invitation to lunch.

CHAPTER NINETEEN

Fred suggested Wednesday for lunch, so I was able to turn my white lie to Anthea into the truth. He'd suggested we meet at a country-house hotel on the outskirts of Bristol, and as I drove through Henbury I was wondering how to introduce the subject I wanted to talk to him about. There seemed no immediately obvious way, so I decided to leave it to chance and see how the conversation went.

It was a very pleasant place, and Fred was obviously an old and valued customer because we were welcomed with enthusiasm and given the best table — by the window overlooking well-kept parkland that even at this time of the year looked very pleasant.

"Shall I order for us both?" Fred asked. "I've worked my way through the menus here many times and I think I know which are the chef's special dishes."

"That will be lovely," I said.

When the waiter, who'd been hovering solicitously as we took our seats, had taken the order. Fred continued. "So sorry Estelle couldn't be here today, but she's in Antibes opening up the apartment." He smiled at my questioning look. "I really can't face an English winter any more and I certainly can't face an English Christmas and New Year these days."

"What about Charlie?" I asked. "Does he join you?"

"Sometimes, but this year he's in Los Angeles."

"Really?"

"Yes, he's a theatrical agent now in partnership with his friend Geoffrey Bailey — they have quite a few well-known clients. Charlie's in LA to fix up a movie deal for one of them." He mentioned a popular film actor even I had heard of.

"Goodness, he has done well!"

"Well, he's got his head screwed on — he realized pretty soon that he was never going to make it as an actor, but he had all the contacts and — even if I say it myself — he's inherited my business sense, so he's done pretty well. It helped that Jessica has a lot of theatrical friends, of course, and he met most of them when he was living with her. Mothers do have their uses. Ah, here's the terrine — I think you'll enjoy this."

It was certainly delicious, and so was the exquisitely cooked turbot that followed it. All through the meal Fred kept up a flow of interesting conversation and anecdotes about well-known personalities that he seemed to be on friendly terms with. When the dessert arrived ("There's nothing quite like a perfect crème brûlée, don't you agree?"), he began to talk about my mother and father — stories of their younger days — and how much he admired them both.

"I was much younger than them, of course," he said, "and really a boring young idiot in many ways, but they always treated me as an equal, in experience and intelligence. I watched you and Jeremy grow up and envied you your parents."

He was silent for a moment. "My mother died when I was quite young, so I was more or less left to nurses and housekeepers. I didn't see much of my father. He was a wonderful man, but he was totally absorbed in the business and wasn't home much. Then, of course, I was away at school — I enjoyed it really; I've always found it easy to make friends. But, of course, it wasn't the same as family."

"Your father," I said tentatively, "he was very successful, wasn't he?"

"Oh, yes. My grandfather built the business up from nothing — engineering, you may remember — and both my father and his younger brother worked for him. But my uncle wasn't that interested, so, when their father died, my father bought him out and he went to New Zealand to keep sheep or some such thing."

"I never knew there was a brother," I said. "I don't remember him from Bernard's family tree."

Fred pushed back his chair and regarded me quizzically. "Oh, you've seen that, have you?"

"He did one for each branch of the family, and, actually, when he died, Janet passed his notes and research things on to me."

"I see. So you've seen the notes?"

"Yes," I said, feeling rather embarrassed now that it had actually come to the point. "I looked through all the notes and things. For all the branches of the family," I added hastily.

Fred smiled. "So you discovered our particular skeleton?" I hesitated and Fred continued. "Oh, come on, you can't have missed it. My father being born out of wedlock, as they used to say. He was two years old when my grandparents married. Trust Bernard to dig that out!"

"He seems," I said, "to have managed to find out something about every branch of the family that they'd have preferred to keep hidden."

"Not your branch?"

"Well, no, as it happens, and not Hilda's — you know what she's like; she sent him away with a very sharp warning not to meddle — but practically everyone else."

"He really was a nasty little creep."

"Did it upset you," I asked, "finding out like that?"

Fred laughed. "Oh, we'd all known for ages, part of the family legend. It's rather a touching story and quite unusual for that time. My grandmother's father was a widower, a very eccentric man, and she was his only daughter. He was suffering from consumption and obviously hadn't long to live. In those days, daughters were expected to live at home and look after their invalid parents, and my grandmother was very fond of him, but she was in her thirties when she met my father, and not surprisingly they felt that time was going by. But her father wouldn't agree to their marriage. Even though they promised to live with him and look after him, he was adamant about it. I suppose he had a superstitious feeling that if there was an actual ceremony he couldn't be sure that she'd stay. Stupid, really, but that's the way he felt. The amazing thing was, he suggested that my grandfather should move into the house and live with my grandmother as if they *were* married."

"Good heavens."

"I know. I said he was eccentric. Anyway, my father was born — and christened. I suppose that's the 'evidence' Bernard found, and then the later marriage certificate."

"Well, yes. What an amazing story. But surely there must have been a terrific scandal — your grandparents living together without being married?"

"Oh, it was given out that they'd been married, quietly in London, and then, of course, when my great-grandfather finally died, that's exactly what they did. It was pretty clever of Bernard, tracking *that* down."

"He was very thorough."

"Yes, he was that. Probably the only acceptable quality he had. He was a really nasty piece of work — but I expect you've discovered that for yourself."

I nodded. "Before all this — all the genealogy business — I'd never seen much of him. We all just thought of him as a terrific bore to be avoided at all cost. But now . . ."

"Now you know a bit more?"

"The awful way he treated Janet and poor Luke and — well, so many things!"

The waiter brought the coffee and I was amused to see that he set the tray down in front of Fred for him to pour out.

"Oh, yes," Fred said, pushing down the plunger of the cafetière, "he was a genuine twenty-four-carat bastard." He poured the coffee neatly and passed the jug of cream to me. "That's why I went to his funeral — just to make sure he'd gone."

"I'm so glad," I said, "that he didn't cause any sort of upset in your family with all his 'research.' "

Fred smiled. "No — though I can well believe he'd have wanted to. I was glad my father told me all those years ago. It helped, in a way, to understand why he felt compelled to make such a success, why he devoted all his time to the business — I suppose he felt he had something to prove. Ridiculous really, but people do and feel the oddest things. Now, *I* have no wish at all to prove anything, and, of course, I've never had to. There's always been a lot of money — even after Jessica's settlement and getting Charlie started!"

"Lucky you!"

"Yes, I have been, haven't I? And I've really enjoyed my life, especially now I've got

Estelle. I hope you're happy too, Sheila."

I smiled. "Obviously things have never been the same since Peter died, but in other ways I've been very lucky, and, yes, I am happy."

Fred smiled again. "Good," he said. "And now I'm going to tell you something that will make you even happier."

"Really?"

"The best thing about all Bernard's digging back into the family tree is the fact that he wasn't a Prior at all."

"What!"

"Not just not a Prior, but not even English."

"No!"

"His parents couldn't have children — tried for ages with no luck — so when they were living in France (his father was attached to the Paris branch of his bank for several years), they adopted a baby there. Pretended it was their own."

"Really? But how did you know?"

"My mother knew Bernard's mother quite well — knew her before she was married, actually — so she heard all about it. They wanted it kept quiet — I can't think why, but there you are — and so my mother never told anyone, except my father, of course. He told me, years later, when I was grown-up. He mentioned it quite casually; I can't remember in what connection, but he obviously didn't think it was any big deal. I suppose he wasn't that interested."

"Did Bernard know?"

"Oh, yes."

"But no one else?"

"He was very keen to keep it a secret. I think he felt it diminished him in some way — weird!"

"So Janet never knew?"

"Good heavens, no. I did consider telling her after Bernard died, but then I thought, what's the point? Do feel free, though, to tell anyone you like."

I laughed. "I must say, I would be tempted!"

As I drove back along the motorway I played with the idea of spreading the news — it would certainly give a certain grim satisfaction to Veronica and others that Bernard had injured — but I decided that only my cousin Hilda would appreciate the full irony of the situation, so she would be the only one I would tell, apart, that is, from Michael, Thea and Rosemary, whom I tell everything.

It was beginning to get dark by the time I got home (the evenings were drawing in), but I felt I had to let the animals out since they'd been in all day. Tris did his usual tour of the garden, announcing his presence to any animal marauder by short barks, but he came in quite quickly, eager for supper. Foss, however, vanished completely and even an hour later still hadn't come back. I wandered round the garden in the dark calling him and rattling the tin his treats are kept in, but to no avail. He does this sometimes, a punishment for being shut up all day, and I suppose I ought to be used to it by now, but if you're silly about animals you never do get used to it, and so I got a snack (I really didn't need much supper after that large lunch) and sat by the television, eating it without any appetite, getting up at frequent intervals to see whether he'd come back, and calling again, though with little hope. Finally, after another hour, when I was washing up my plate and glass, Tris, who'd accompanied me into the kitchen in case there was the chance of more food, looked at the back door and gave a little whine. And, of course, when I opened the door, Foss strolled nonchalantly in ("Have you been calling me?") and stood beside his dish expecting me to feed him. I thought how furious I'd have been if a person had treated me that way, but there I was, overwhelmed with relief, putting food in his dish and saying stupid things like "You came in! *Good* boy!" After all that, I was fit only for an early night and a soothing read of *Pillars of the House*.

Denzil phoned the next morning about measuring up the stairs for the new carpet.

"I can fit you in this afternoon, if you like, Mrs. Malory. I could do you on my way home, about five fifteen, if that's all right."

He didn't take long to do the measuring, even hampered by Foss, who considers the stairs his own particular domain and sat resolutely on each stair, obstructing Denzil as he worked his way down. When it was finished he said that, yes, a cup of tea would be very nice, thank you. So we sat in the kitchen and he told me about how his girlfriend wanted them to go to Crete for a holiday but he was saving up for a new bike.

"What sort have you got?" I asked.

"It's a 750 Kawasaki."

"Oh, my son had one of those, though his was only a 400. He loved it and hated getting rid of it, but he really did need a car."

"That's what Denise wants me to get," Denzil said, sighing heavily. "She says she's sick of being out in all weathers on the back of the bike."

"But you still want another bike? What

sort — a Harley?"

"No." Denzil considered the point carefully. "Your Harley's a marvelous bike, and so's your big BMW, but, no, the bike I want is something really special."

"Oh?"

"It's a Laverda, an Italian job. There's not many of *those* about. You'd feel pretty special riding one of them! And," he went on, warming to his theme, "perfect for the roads down here, the way it performs on the bends — you could get from here to Bridgwater in half an hour!"

"A Laverda," I said. "I believe I know someone who has one of those."

"Really? Not local, is he?"

"No, he lives in Bristol."

"I thought he wouldn't be local — I'd know if he was. Like I said, they're pretty rare. That's why I was so surprised to see one that night."

"What do you mean?"

"It was a dreadful night, wind and rain, and I was late, so I took the back road to Dunster, and I don't know if you know it — there's a sort of layby just before you get to the lane that runs up to where those holiday cottages are. Anyway, as I went by I saw this Laverda parked there. I couldn't believe my eyes. I'd have stopped and had a proper look, but, like I said, I was late and I had to get on. Funny thing, though, seeing it there, just like that."

"When was this? Do you remember?"

"It was the twenty-third of last month — semifinal of the skittles tournament; that's where I was going."

"What time would that have been?"

"Oh" — he thought for a moment — "it would have been just after a quarter to nine. Yes, that's it; I needed to be at the Red Lion in Dunster by nine — I'm on the skittles team and I was in the last session — and I was running late. Like I said, if it hadn't been for that, I'd have stopped and had a good look at that Laverda." He looked at me inquiringly and I felt obliged to make some excuse for my cross-questioning.

"I just wondered," I said, "if by any chance the bike could have belonged to my friend, but he wouldn't have been there then."

Denzil finished his tea and got up. "Right, then, I'll be getting along. Mr. Davis says he'll have to order the carpet you want, but it shouldn't be long. We'll give you a ring when it's in, and I'll try and fit you in as soon as possible. Thanks for the tea."

After he'd gone I sat for a long time, try-ing to make sense of what he'd told me. I was quite sure that the bike Denzil had seen belonged to Luke. But Luke had telephoned Christine from the restaurant just before eight — she'd been quite positive about that — and even on a Laverda, there was no way he could have got all the way from Bristol in three-quarters of an hour. Anyway, he'd been in the restaurant cooking delicious meals for his regular customers. But somehow I knew that Luke *had* been there.

On an impulse I picked up the telephone and dialed Janet's number.

"Sheila, how lovely to hear from you. I do hope we can get together soon; there's so much going on here. It's so exciting; I long to tell you all about it."

"Actually," I said, "I would rather like to come and see you. There's something I want to talk to you about."

"Oh. Really?" Her voice lost its enthusiastic note and she sounded wary.

"Would tomorrow be too soon? About eleven?"

"Yes," she said, "that would be fine."

I put the phone down and went back into the kitchen, emptied the teapot, and washed up the two cups and saucers, trying not to think too much about what I wanted to say to Janet tomorrow.

Chapter Twenty

When I arrived, I found that Luke was there too.

"Wasn't that lucky," Janet said brightly. "Luke's just dropped in to bring me some of his marvelous cheesecake, and when he heard you were coming he said he'd stay and say hello. Do sit down. Would you like some coffee — and a piece of the cheesecake, of course?"

"Hello, Luke," I said. "You didn't come on your bike, then? At least I didn't see it outside."

"No." He gave me a slight, nervous smile. "I walked — the restaurant's not far from here. I need the exercise."

"It certainly is a remarkable bike," I went on, "in the sense, that is, of being remarked upon. On the night of the twenty-third of last month, for example, in the layby near the holiday cottage." There was an almost palpable silence. I waited for a moment and then went on. "I don't know how you managed it, not with that very firm alibi, but I'm quite sure it was you who tried to kill your father."

"No, Sheila, no!" Janet tried to get to her feet, but Luke quietly restrained her, and they sat side by side on the sofa, facing me.

"Well, Luke," I said, "am I right?"

He nodded. "Yes, quite right."

"It wasn't what you think," Janet said, becoming more agitated. "It was my fault, not Luke's — you must believe that!"

Luke put his hand over hers. "It's all right," he said soothingly. "I'll tell her. I'll explain everything."

"I think I can understand why you did it," I said. "I just can't work out how."

"Well, you know how things have been," Luke said, "and they were getting worse. He discovered that Mother and I had been meeting secretly. There was a terrible row and he forbade her to see me ever again. It was very difficult — he hardly let her out of his sight — but she did manage to phone me a couple of times. I tried to persuade her to leave him and come to us, Yves and me, but she was too frightened."

"He would have tried to destroy them," Janet broke in. "He said he could have the restaurant closed down, things like that, if I went away."

"Rubbish, of course," Luke said, "but enough to frighten her. It couldn't go on like that. There was only one thing to be done. Mother told me they were going down to Taviscombe for a bit and it seemed like an ideal opportunity to get rid of him once and for all. The moment Mother saw a chance of a perfect alibi for herself, I'd come down and — and do it."

"He liked to spend the evenings going over his notes," Janet said. She seemed to have recovered her composure and spoke quite calmly. "So, even before he complained of being ill during the day, I'd arranged with Luke that I'd take the things round to you that evening."

"We — that is, I — had got it all planned. Mother took the key of the cottage and had a copy made in Taviscombe one day when she was doing the shopping; then she put it in an envelope and sent it to me. I was to let myself in, and then, when I'd done it, I was going to break a window and make it look like a burglary that had gone wrong."

"I'd got a mobile phone," Janet said. "The man in the shop showed me how to use it. Bernard didn't know I had it, of course. As soon as I got into the taxi I phoned Luke on his mobile and let him know that I'd left the house."

"And you started out then?" I asked Luke.

"No. I was well on my way by then," he said. "I was at Brent Knoll service station waiting until a quarter to eight, when I phoned Christine." He smiled. "I phoned her from the cafe there and said I was phoning from my restaurant. One lot of restaurant noises sounds very like any other."

"That was neat," I said. He gave a sort of nod. "But the rest of your alibi," I went on. "Everyone seems to think you were in the restaurant all night preparing all that marvelous food."

"I'm afraid it wasn't all that marvelous that night," Luke said. "I cooked everything beforehand — casseroles of pheasant and pigeon, made-up dishes like that, things that Yves could warm up in the microwave. I was very upset at having to do that," he said earnestly. "I've always prided myself on everything being freshly prepared. People seemed to accept the food that evening, but it wasn't something I was proud of doing."

"Unlike trying to kill your father?" I suggested. He didn't reply, so I went on. "But you were back at the restaurant before all the customers left."

"That bike is amazing," Luke said. "Perfect for minor roads, takes the bends like a dream — I made fantastic time. Yes, I was back in good time to do my usual round of the restaurant. It's funny how people take things at their face value. They see what they expect to see. I was there at the end of the evening, so they thought I'd been there all the time. Why wouldn't they?"

"I see."

"It was odd," Luke said thoughtfully. "I let myself in with the key, and the lights were on and everything. I didn't really know what to do. I'd been bracing myself for confronting him, having a scene, and then — then killing him. But when I saw him in the chair, asleep as I thought, I was so relieved. I just hit him hard with the heavy mallet I'd brought and got out as fast as I could. I was halfway down the path when I realized I hadn't broken the window and done all the things I was supposed to do to make it look like a burglary. I went out into the back garden, through the kitchen, and did what I had to and left."

"So you didn't go back into the sitting room to make sure your father was dead?"

He shuddered. "Oh, no, I couldn't. I just went back to the bike and got away really fast . . ."

His voice died away and there was silence for a while. Then Janet spoke.

"What are you going to do, Sheila?"

"Do?"

"Are you going to tell the police?"

"Tell them what? You can't be charged with killing Bernard if he was dead already. There may be some sort of charge — conspiracy or something, I really don't know."

"If only we'd waited," Janet said. "Just one more day, then it would have been all right."

"Yes."

"But you do *see*," she said, "how desperate it was, how we had to do something!"

I sighed. "I can see why you thought so."

Luke stood up. "You mustn't blame Mother," he said. "None of it was her fault. You know how it's been."

"Yes," I said, "I know." I stood up too.

"So what *are* you going to do?" he asked.

"I don't know," I said. "I really don't know." I moved to the door. "I'll see myself out."

Janet came quickly towards me and took my arm. "Please, Sheila, *please* don't spoil it all for us."

I shook my arm free and went out, then got into my car and drove away, along the road and up onto the Downs, where I stopped because I was shaking. I turned the engine off and sat there, staring ahead of me but not really seeing anything. I must have stayed like that for a good five minutes; then my mind began to work again and I realized that my main feeling was that of anger. I was furious at the way they'd used me, a perfect alibi for Janet, a witness when she discovered the body. I thought of how upset I'd been for her, how much sympathy and compassion I'd shown her, of the charade that she and Luke had played out when he came to see her after the murder, and all the time . . .

I badly needed something to help me pull myself together. I couldn't face going down into Clifton and trying to find a parking space so that I could get a drink in a pub or a cup of tea in a café. I scrabbled about in the glove compartment and found a rather old bar of chocolate and ate it all. When I'd finished I felt a bit sick, but more able to continue my journey. I put the car radio on and drove back along the motorway with music from blessed Radio 3 blocking out the thoughts I didn't want to consider.

At home I made the cup of tea I'd been longing for and sat for a while, feeling absolutely shattered. Tris and Foss, sensing my mood as they so often did, came and sat beside me on the sofa. I put the television on and watched, mindlessly, a cookery program and some sort of quiz show. After a while I got up and went outside. Walking round the garden, dutifully attended by Tris (Foss had taken one look at the cold, windy weather and remained indoors), I tried to think about things more calmly. I tried to remember the dreadful pressures Luke and Janet had been under, the appalling way Bernard had treated them both, the terrible things he'd done to Alma and her family, and all the unpleasant things about him that had been revealed, and I faced the fact that I too thought the world was a better place without him. I was glad he was dead and couldn't hurt people anymore, but murder? No. As Janet had said, if only they'd waited one more day.

I'd promised to have dinner with Michael and Thea that evening, and as I looked out a bottle of wine to take for them and a picture book for Alice, I thought with a sudden rush of pleasure and gratitude of my own family and how lucky I was. Alice greeted me with enthusiasm and took me off to play Shops, which involved a great deal of rather messy weighing out of lentils and split peas, a proceeding which Alice never seemed to tire of ("Now *I'll* be the shop lady and you be the Mummy doing the shopping"), and I found this repetition was the perfect antidote to the miseries of the day, as was sitting on Alice's bed reading to her for the umpteenth time the adventures of *The Moose on the Moon*.

When we were finally sitting down to Thea's splendid steak and kidney pudding, I exclaimed with pleasure, "Perfect comfort food!"

"Oh, dear," Thea said, "has Alice tired you out? She really can be exhausting!"

"No, it was lovely having time with her — just what I needed, like this delicious steak and kidney. No, it's just that I've had a very difficult day." I told them all about my visit to Janet in Bristol and said, "I really don't know what to do about it."

"Well, you must tell Roger, of course," Michael said. "He needs to know."

"Yes, I suppose he does," I said doubtfully, "and I want to in a way. But I can't help thinking — well, of everything, all the awful things Bernard did to them and to other people. And if Janet and Luke can really start afresh and make a good life for themselves . . ."

"I can see what Sheila means," Thea said. "At least *something* good will have come out of it."

"Of course," I said, "I suppose they shouldn't profit from their crime, or whatever it was."

"Whatever it was," Michael said firmly, "it was wrong and you've got to tell Roger."

So the next evening I rang him at home. In some way I felt it was less official than ringing him at work.

"Oh, sorry, Sheila," Jilly said, "he's away at a conference. Was it important?"

"Not really. It can wait."

"It's in Brussels — something to do with the EU, liaising or some such thing — so he won't be back until next week. Honestly, these conferences are the limit — we hardly ever see him."

"It does sound a bit much."

"Anyway, I'll tell him you want a word. Forgive me if I dash, but I've got to take Delia to a pony sleepover."

"Good heavens, what is that?"

"Riding each other's ponies and staying up all night talking about horses!"

"I didn't know Delia had her own pony."

"She hasn't yet, but it's only a question of time. She's planning to ambush Roger about it when he gets back from Brussels!"

The following day Denzil came and laid the new carpet. I'd shut Tris in the kitchen, where the noise of hammering wouldn't disturb him too much, and Foss I'd firmly put outside, so that a furious chocolate-colored face appeared at each window in turn, trying to find a way in. When it was all done and I was giving Denzil his tea in the kitchen, I said, "What is it to be, a new bike or a car?"

He sighed heavily. "My cousin's got an old Ford he'll let me have cheap — that'll keep Denise quiet, and Mr. Davis says I can have some more overtime, and I can put that towards the bike."

"So what about the holiday?"

"Oh, well, that'll have to go. You can't have everything in this life; that's what I always say."

After he left, I poured myself another cup of tea and was sitting considering this pragmatic philosophy when the phone rang. It was Janet.

"Hello, Sheila; I'd thought I'd give you a quick ring." Her voice was hesitant, almost wary. "We're off to France tomorrow." Fleetingly I wondered why she felt it necessary to inform me about her holiday plans; then she went on. "For good."

"What!"

"We're going to Normandy. Monsieur Picard — I don't know if you remember about him; he owned the restaurant that Luke worked in first of all. Well, Luke's always kept in touch, he was so grateful for the chance he got there. Anyway, Monsieur Picard's getting on now, and he wants to retire. He asked Luke if he'd consider taking over and Luke jumped at it. It's got a very good reputation and they think there's a chance of a Michelin star."

"I see."

"So we're going straightaway." Her voice was brisk now, almost businesslike. "I haven't got probate yet, but I've left the house in the agent's hands. Monsieur Picard is willing to wait until the money comes through. Luke will be a sort of manager until that happens."

"What does Christine think about it?"

There was a slight pause. "I haven't told Christine yet. I'll ring her from France. Luke says there's nothing she can do to stop it."

"I see."

"It's the new start we've all been wanting, Sheila, Luke and Yves and I" — she was coaxing now — "and I couldn't go without letting you know and hoping you'd understand — well, about everything."

"Yes," I said, "I understand. But that doesn't mean that I can condone what you've done."

"No. I suppose not," she said slowly. "Anyway," she went on, "I thought I'd give you our telephone number over there — just in case you ever come to France . . ."

I wrote down the number she gave me, said good-bye, and put the phone down.

As I washed up the teacups I decided that Janet would always be a puzzle to me — such a contradictory mixture, I really didn't know what to make of her and probably never would. The telephone call did, however, confirm my decision to tell Roger everything I knew. And I would give him the telephone number.

My thoughts were interrupted by a ring at the door. Feeling that quite enough had happened for one morning, I went to answer it reluctantly, but to my delight it was Rosemary in a state of great excitement.

"I had to come and tell you right away," she said, hardly waiting until she'd got inside the door. "I'm so thrilled!"

"Come and sit down," I said, "and tell me."

"It's about the ruby wedding," she said.

"Have you finally decided where to have it?"

"No, no," she said impatiently, "it's better than that."

She fished in her handbag and brought out a folder and handed it to me. Inside were two airline tickets to Toronto.

"No!" I said. "What a wonderful surprise! Not Jack?"

"Yes, bless him. He thought of it all by himself (though Jilly did the actual booking for him) because he saw how sad I was not to be able to see baby John and meet Marianne. So he rang Colin and said we'd be there for the christening."

"How absolutely brilliant!"

"And," Rosemary went on, "he said that since we were going all that way we might as well stay over for Christmas."

"Jack!"

"I know, isn't it unbelievable!"

A thought struck me. "What about your mother? Is she furious?"

"That's the extraordinary thing. She's *pleased.*"

"I don't believe it!"

"No, she said it was for the *family* and it was our duty to be there for the christening."

"Good heavens."

"Mind you, she still expects a splendid meal at the Castle when we get back, with Jilly, Roger and the children." She smiled. "And you, of course; after all, you were my bridesmaid all those years ago."

"That would be lovely. Oh I'm *so* pleased. It's the perfect solution."

"Anyway, can you come with me to Taunton next week and help me buy some baby clothes to take with us?"

"Of course."

As I came back from seeing her out, a familiar sound caught my attention. There, his head turned to make sure I was watching, Foss was energetically sharpening his claws on the new stair carpet.

ABOUT THE AUTHOR

Hazel Holt was a personal friend and literary adviser to Barbara Pym, and is Pym's official biographer. A former television critic and feature writer, she lives in Somerset, England.